2

A DARK MAFIA ARRANGED MARRIAGE ROMANCE

HEARTLESS

Vows

USA Today Bestselling Author
V.T. BONDS

Copyright © 2024 by V.T. Bonds

Cover by GetCovers.

All rights reserved.

No part of this book may be reproduced in any form or by any electronic or mechanical means, including information storage and retrieval systems, without written permission from the author, except for the use of brief quotations in a book review.

Go to https://vtbonds.com for a complete list of books by V.T. Bonds.

For new releases, discounts, and Knotty Exclusives, subscribe to V.T. Bonds' newsletter at

https://vtbonds.com/newslettersubscriber.

I legit ate my way through writing this story, so this one goes to all the coffee, energy drinks, sushi, and snacks I decimated while pounding away on the keyboard.

Also, fuck you, strep, flu, and covid. You suck. Leave my kids alone.

CONTENTS

CHAPTER 1

Aurora Achilles

WHEN MY PARENTS' SCREAMING no longer echoes down the hall, I confirm the funds hit my account with a glance, exit out of the browser, maximize my secondary browser with my college work already loaded, and pull my headphones over my ears. My father slams the door to his study. A few seconds later, my phone lights up and vibrates beside my keyboard. As the lock on my door rattles, I open the top drawer of my desk and pull out my over-the-counter medicines before standing and grabbing my prescription off my bookcase.

My mother scoffs from the doorway.

"What's the point of hiding your medicine? It's not like your brother can wander through the house, and even if he could, he wouldn't dare set foot in your room," she says.

I bite my tongue and systematically take out one pill from each bottle as she watches.

It's her fault my eight-year-old brother tiptoes around like a ghost in his own home. Anger writhes in my veins, but fear keeps me silent.

My stomach sours as she steps into my room and fills it with her cloying perfume, but I ignore the fear skittering down my spine and pivot to show her the cluster of pills on my palm.

She nods. I pop them into my mouth, take a swig of water, and swallow before showing her my empty tongue.

"Give me the bottle," she demands with an impatient flick of her wrist toward the bookshelf.

I place my water back onto my desk and pass the prescription to her. She pops it open and sneers before closing and tossing it back at me.

"Are you turning work in late? Didn't you graduate last week?"

I follow her glare to my computer screen and swallow my apprehension before shaking my head.

"I started college courses last semester," I partially lie.

She doesn't need to know I forged her and my father's approval for college classes several years ago. Graduating from high school on time is a farce, too, since I finished all my classes long ago, but delaying my diploma is probably the only reason I'm still under their roof.

I can't leave. Not yet. Not when Tristan is still so young and vulnerable.

"What major?" she asks as she leans down and squints at my screen.

"Business administration," I respond.

It's another half lie. I earned my associate degree in business administration early last year, but only because it looks good on a résumé. My passion lies in technology, and even though what they teach in college is insultingly basic compared to what I've learned on my own, having the official paperwork under my name will further my plan for freedom. I'm only a few credits away from my bachelor's degree in computer science.

My mother huffs and turns toward the door.

"Fine, but you'd better not let your classes interfere with real life. We're going to have a busy summer."

Her threat rings through my ears as she slams the door behind her. I push my headphones down around my neck and rub the ache between my eyes as she locks my door and stomps down the hallway.

When she pauses next to Tristan's door, I stiffen and grab my phone. With trembling fingers, I open my parental app and monitor the sounds in his room until she walks away.

I sigh in relief and close my eyes for a moment. When my chest finally stops aching, I send Tristan a heart through text and smile when he responds with a vomit emoji. After a quick *go to sleep* message, I set down my phone, submit my work to my professor, and minimize the page.

My phone vibrates. Dozens of z's fill my screen. I chuckle, shake my head, and engage downtime on his computer, but extend his access on his phone for an extra fifteen minutes. I pull up a separate browser on my computer but wait until the faint sound of rushing water comes through my phone speaker before filtering the offers waiting in my inbox.

I'm no longer desperate for money, but the more I have in my account, the less I worry, so I'll continue snagging the higher paying, quick turnaround online jobs as often as I can.

Less than five minutes later, Tristan's shower turns off. I sigh and accept an offer before picking up my phone and sending my brother a toothbrush emoji. A few seconds later, he sends me a blurry photo of his reflection in his bathroom mirror with white foam dripping down his chin.

I blink back unexpected tears and breathe through the sudden lump in my throat.

He's growing too fast. I upload the photo to my hidden cloud but delete it from our conversation—and every official record—before sending him a thumbs up.

Two minutes later, he wishes me goodnight. I end our conversation with a kiss emoji. My app alerts me as he opens his favorite game on his phone.

With half my attention on his app usage, I accept a job and halfway complete it before his phone locks him out. His grumbling as he settles into bed assures me he's a healthy eight-year-old boy.

I finish the job and submit it for approval before closing the browser and logging into a program of my own making.

My heart skips a beat as a new device pops on screen. I scroll through the short call log and plug the phone numbers into the database I've been building for years.

After skimming through the conversations, I decide none of the information is worth transcribing and zip the files under today's date before skimming through my mother's tablet and phone usage. When I find nothing out of the ordinary, I pause long enough to pop a piece of gum in my mouth and let the blast of mint clear my head before I sneak into my father's phone.

Three new contacts. Half a dozen new email addresses. Four accepted calls from numbers without contact information.

My stomach churns. I choose the longest call, fit my headphones over my ears, and brace my elbows on my desk.

Surprise flares through me as a woman's voice comes through the speakers, but as the conversation unfolds, disgust supersedes all else. Ignoring my growing nausea, I transcribe the entire interaction and file it away before jumping into detective mode.

After a few minutes of typing, I successfully hack one of the unknown numbers from my father's call log—a burner phone bought from a corner store on the other side of the city—and use the already-disposed-of-device to send an anonymous tip to my local police station.

I wipe my sweaty hands on my thighs and silently curse myself. Tipping off the police isn't part of my plan. I can't keep taking unnecessary risks, but the thought of doing nothing fills me with guilt.

Some things my family thrives off—like drugs, weapons, and money laundering—I can ignore, since they rarely involve innocent people, but my father has grown less scrupulous over the years. I ruined his last attempt at human trafficking. I'll do it again, if I must.

If my escape plans fall through and this is the only way I can protect Tristan, at least he won't inherit an empire built on innocent women's misfortune.

I'm not an idiot. Escaping the mafia lifestyle, especially from one of New York City's founding families, is unlikely.

But I have to try.

I exit out of all my hacking programs and replace my history with a randomized list of presets and times before checking my inbox, sending the second half of my open job, and confirming the funds hit my account before closing down for the night.

I stumble through my nightly hygiene routine and snag my phone off my desk before dropping into bed. Right before I slip into a doze, my phone buzzes. I check the screen and grab the hairpins from my bedside table before tucking my phone into my pocket and rising.

With a few practiced moves, I pick the lock on my door and tiptoe down the hall to Tristan's room. I pick his lock without turning on a light and ease his door closed behind me. I whisper his name. He whimpers and curls into a tighter ball. I settle onto the bed behind him and rub his back.

"Hush, Tristan, I'm here. You're okay. No one can hurt you," I whisper.

He wakes with a sob and rolls over to bury his face against my chest. I gather him to me and stroke his hair from his face.

He's no longer the tiny newborn whose entire body fits on my torso, but he's still my little brother. I'll do anything for him. I wish I could take away his nightmares, but at least he doesn't remember why he has them, and part of me is grateful I'm not alone. Even with star-shaped lights dancing across his ceiling from the lamp on his bedside table and his warm yet bony eight-year-old body curled against mine, I struggle to fall asleep as memories of the worst night of my life plague me.

I decide to stay with Tristan all night instead of going back and forth between our rooms, so I regulate my breathing until my body follows my cues and drops into regenerative sleep.

I grunt awake when Tristan's bony elbow digs into my stomach.

"You're in here again?" he mumbles as he sits up and rubs his eyes.

I groan and throw my arm over my face.

"Did I have another nightmare?" he asks.

I shrug and roll away from him.

"Ari, why're you in here?"

His little hands push and pull at my shoulders.

"Did you spy on me again?"

I sigh and give a halfhearted, blind swat behind me.

"Give me a few minutes to wake up before you grill me, will ya?"

"You did spy, didn't you!"

I shrug again and bury my face in his pillow.

"Why're you always spying on me? Get out of my room," he demands as he shoves my shoulder a few more times.

"What if mamma comes looking for you?"

I sigh and force myself to sit up.

"For real, though, did I wake you up in the middle of the night again?"

The worry in his tone wipes away the last traces of sleep. I shake my head and push my hair back from my face.

"No, you didn't wake me. I hadn't gone to sleep yet."

"Ari!" His little hand whacks my leg with enough force to sting. I hiss and rub the spot. "You need to go to bed earlier. You can't get sick again."

"What do you mean *again*? You were only two the last time, so there's no way you remember anything except what mamma told you. Stop letting her get to you."

"Whatever! You were so pale and floppy when that man picked you up. I thought you were dead."

My heart clenches. I hide my emotions behind a faux upset.

"Did you just call me floppy?"

His mouth flattens even as mirth glints in his eyes.

"Don't you dare," he growls.

I flop onto my belly across his bed like an oversized rag doll, spreading my limbs and taking up as much space as I can. He pushes my arm off his lap. I dig my fingers into his side.

We devolve into chaos and giggles until his alarm rings. I stumble to my feet and toss his blanket back onto the bed.

"Alright! Playtime's over. Get ready for tutoring," I say, and chuck a pillow at his head when he groans.

"No complaining. I booked Mr. Hearthright every day this week."

At my announcement, he perks up and catches the second pillow with ease.

"Will Adam and Taylor be there, too?"

I nod. His smile warms my soul.

"Thanks, big sis," he says before bouncing into the bathroom.

Trusting him to get ready on his own, since he'll basically be hanging out with his best friends and going on outlandish field trips with the eclectic and highly sought after private glorified babysitter every day for the next seven days, I slip into the hallway, lock his door behind me, and secure myself into my room before dropping the hair pins back into their jar.

With an unsettled sigh, I run my hands through my hair and walk into my bathroom.

I haven't had an episode in six years, but I suppose if Tristan has night terrors about what happened when he was barely a week old, he could also remember seeing me faint. Guilt creeps through me. I'll never let myself get so weak again. He shouldn't have to worry about whether I can care for him.

With my resolve firmed, I change into gym clothes, tie my hair back, and slap on just enough makeup to appease my mother before tossing my purse into my duffle bag. I add a few extra protein bars into a side pocket and choose the least disgusting one for an early breakfast teaser and choke it down with half a bottle of water.

When my mother unlocks my door, I offer her my normal greeting. She eyes me with bleary contempt and shuffles down the hall without a word.

I wait until she slams her door behind her before I swing my duffle over my shoulder and scurry to Tristan's room.

He bounces on the balls of his feet as I open his door.

"Hurry, she's grumpy," I whisper.

He closes his mouth with an invisible zipper and tosses the imaginary key over his shoulder. I place a kiss on his forehead and usher him down the stairs without another word.

We say good morning to the chef and eat toast and eggs—and my favorite morning spinach mix—while sitting at the bar as he prepares for my mother's more elaborate meal. Before she glides down the stairs, I rush him out the front door, shake hands with Mr. Hearthright, and wave goodbye as our driver maneuvers the SUV through the front gates.

I turn around and freeze at the sight of my mother standing in the front doorway. She summons me into the ornate dining room with a tilt of her head and perches in her normal seat at the table as I drop my duffle on the floor beside the wall and settle in the seat beside her.

"You'll meet your betrothed today."

My entire body locks in shock. I stare at her as my brain struggles to process her words.

"He needs an heir. You'll agree to give him one. Don't speak a single fucking word otherwise, or you'll never see your brother again."

I blink and wonder what hellhole I fell into this morning.

She scoffs, picks up her steaming coffee, and glares at me out of the corner of her eye.

"What do you say, Aurora?"

I swallow but can't force myself to respond.

"Don't pretend this is a shock. You're eighteen now. This was going to happen eventually."

She sips her coffee and leans toward me. The evil gleam in her eyes curdles my stomach. I flick my attention between her face and the scalding coffee as it teases the rim of her mug. Just before it escapes onto my arm, I nod.

"Yes, ma'am. I understand."

As my father's footsteps sound on the stairs, she sneers, sets down her drink, and demands I be presentable by lunchtime before shooing me away.

I grab my duffle and escape out the side door without greeting my father. As I approach the car, the bulky driver snaps to attention and rushes to open my door for me. I thank him and request a ride to the gym as I drop into my seat.

He shuts the door, closing me in deafening silence as my mind reels from my mother's decree. I press my palms over my eyes, uncaring about my makeup, and take several calming breaths before staring out the window in mute shock as the world rolls by.

Nothing matters so long as Tristan is safe. I don't even care who I'm marrying, why an heir is so important to them, or how dangerous it'll be for me to be pregnant. All I need is more time. Just a little more time.

My pep talk doesn't work.

HEARTLESS VOWS

Dread builds in my chest.

MARRIAGE VOWS

CHAPTER 2

Giorgio Vivaldi

I TOSS THE BLOODY KNIFE on the table with the other rusty tools and wipe my hands on the white rag but grimace as it smears sticky crimson over my skin. With an angry snarl, I fling the useless fabric onto my latest victim's face and stomp to the adjacent room—the abandoned diner's kitchen—to wash my hands.

Fiero chuckles and leans against the counter, far out of my reach.

"You did this on purpose, didn't you? You fucking *stronzo*," I snarl.

He crosses his arms over his chest and gives a smug shrug.

"Serves you right for not checking your surroundings before you started slicing and dicing," he says.

I roll my eyes and lather up to my elbows before rinsing the last of the suds from my arms. When I start a second round of scrubbing, my closest and most annoying friend sighs and stands with a shake of his head.

"I'm guessing they didn't tell you what you wanted to hear?" he remarks.

"You'd know if you'd stayed in the room," I growl.

"No man who values his balls would stay in eyesight when you go feral with a knife," he responds.

I sneer and meet his gaze.

"They hurt my family, Fiero."

The nonchalance disappears from his countenance.

"I know," he says as he stands and drops his arms to his sides.

"They raped and beat Camilla until she tried to kill herself."

I can't breathe through the fury and guilt squeezing my chest. I'll never forgive myself for not being there when my older sister needed me most.

"They did," he responds.

I step toward him. He stands his ground, never dropping eye contact despite my intensity.

"They kidnapped Serenity and attacked Nico Russo. My younger sister almost had to raise her child without its father," I say through gritted teeth.

"I know," he says.

I pull my knife from my belt and hold it on my upturned palm in front of me. Fiero's unflinching response solidifies my belief in him. I trust him with my life.

"They will feel every inch of this knife as I sink it into their body over and over *and over again*," I promise.

"They will," he confirms.

Unable to find fault in his response yet too dissatisfied with my ineptitude, I press the tip of the knife to my outer forearm and apply the barest pressure, proving how deadly sharp I keep my blade as fresh crimson flows down my arm, creating new designs within my intricate tattoos.

"I will *slice and dice,*" I emphasize his ridiculous choice of words, "until they beg for mercy, but they'll find I don't have any. They'll tell me their deepest, darkest secrets, and I still won't stop. They'll scream and cry and plead, but I'll just keep cutting even when they beg for death."

"You will," Fiero says with the same cold conviction now condensed behind my sternum.

"Everyone will know it's a mistake to fuck with the Vivaldi family," I vow.

"They already do," he says.

Despite the certainty in his dark eyes, I don't believe him.

"It's been six months since Camilla's attack. Six months of no leads. Six months of these *teste di cazzo* running free. Six months of—"

"Terror. Six months of pure terror. For six months, you've tortured every *stronzo* stupid enough to stick his head up. No one with half a brain will step a toe out of line when everyone knows you're on a hate-fueled warpath," he deadpans.

I freeze and dig the knife a little deeper into my flesh, using the sting to center myself.

Because he's right. The *bastardo* is right.

"It's not just you, either. Nico Russo razed an entire block just to snuff out threats."

I grind my teeth and twist my blade to renew the pain.

"That wasn't Nico. It was Serenity and me. Nico was still in hospital."

Fiero tilts his head and quirks a brow.

"And you waited until now to tell me?"

"I couldn't recruit any of our men. We couldn't leave traces back to the Vivaldi family, since it was in Russo territory. They weren't married yet, and my father wouldn't have approved." I pull the blade from my arm and return to the sink. As I dip my knife under the still flowing faucet, I meet Fiero's glare over my shoulder. "Serenity didn't want Nico involved until he was back on his feet, but with his second and third also in the hospital, she needed help."

"So you cut me out?"

"There was nothing to cut you out of. I couldn't even be there," I snarl as I shake the water from my blade.

Droplets land on my white shirt. I grunt in annoyance as I spot a tiny speck of red near my waistline.

A plume of dust rises from the counter as Fiero flops my garment bag on top. He knows me so well. He snagged it from my trunk and hid it near the doorway as I questioned the poor souls no longer alive in the other room.

I grunt in thanks and dry my blade on my pantleg before unzipping my bag and setting my knife on the open flap to preserve its cleanliness.

Fiero chooses a new counter to lean on as I unroll my sleeves and unbutton my shirt.

"So what's next, boss?" he asks.

I shrug my shirt off my shoulders and drop it onto the flap before pulling my undershirt over my head.

"Should I keep bringing you dead men walking, or is it time for a new strategy?"

I unfasten my belt and meet his eyes as I pull it through my belt loops.

"Are you sure you don't want to be my consigliere? My uncle will always side with my father. I could use you in—"

"Nope. I like the dirty work. All the posturing and backstabbing ain't for me," he interrupts.

I shuck my trousers down my legs, leaving my underwear in place, and work them over my shoes before adding them to the pile of dirty clothes.

"That's a shame, since you're so good at stabbing me in the back," I retort.

"How the hell did your delusional ass come to that conclusion? I've never stabbed you in the back," he says.

"You let me rampage for six months before you said anything."

"I like my balls attached to my body, thank you very much."

He has a point. I haven't been receptive to criticism recently.

"Besides, we get along so well because we handle shit head on. Eye to eye. Straight and to the point. Stabbing in the back is so unsatisfying."

Yet another point in his favor. I wash my face, arms, and chest in the sink again before yanking a few baby wipes from the container in the bottom of my bag and running them over my legs. Once I'm satisfied no blood hides within my tattoos, I shake out the towel rolled at the base of my bag and dry from head to toe before pulling on a fresh pair of trousers.

"Pause the deliveries for now," I decide.

He nods. I slap a bandage over the tiny cut on my arm, pull an undershirt over my head, and settle it in place before threading my arms into a button down. As I systematically fasten my buttons, he waits in silence.

When I open my mouth to speak, my phone buzzes in the pocket of my old pants. I curse and fish it out of the fabric before checking the screen.

I answer my father's call with a curt greeting. The tenseness of his tone lifts the hairs on my nape. He ends the call after I voice my understanding.

I stick the phone in my new pants pocket and add my keys and other things from the old pair before tucking in my shirts and fastening the front.

"Expect a call after I figure out what my father wants," I say as I thread my belt through the loops and close the buckle.

"You got it, boss," Fiero quips.

His insistence on remaining a nameless soldier only solidifies my conviction that he'd be amazing as my second-in-command.

Removing my suit coat from the hanger, I pull it on and smooth the lapels before slipping my knife into my belt and closing my garment bag. Dressed in clean clothes and ready for whatever menial crap my father throws my way, I lift the bag from the counter—careful to hold it away from my outfit—and stalk through the building to the side door.

Fiero knows the drill. He'll ensure we leave nothing behind.

Yet again, he's perfect consigliere material, if he'd just get his head out of his ass and see reason.

I toss the bag into my trunk and slide into the driver's seat before pulling away from the derelict building and heading directly to my familial home. My senses heighten as weight settles onto my shoulders. Driving through the ornate gates only increases the guilt lodged in the pit of my stomach.

Even though I'll inherit the entire estate, I haven't considered this my home in years. It feels more like a job—or rather an unwanted responsibility I can't escape—so I bought a multi-family townhouse near our work building and outfitted it for increased safety.

Self-hatred curdles my stomach. If I had welcomed my sisters into my home instead of selfishly keeping my private space to myself, would their futures look less bleak than they do now?

As the thought crosses my mind, I push it aside. Serenity and Nico are happy. Dwelling on what ifs only leaves a man trapped in the past.

I must remain in the present—with my sights on the future—for the sake of my family. My parents have survived the cutthroat world, but it's time for me to take over and accept responsibility, no matter how reluctant my father is to step down.

Fiero may not have said it directly, but he hinted at the truth. I let my emotions box me in for too long. Now I need to lean into cold, hard calculations.

For my family. My parents. Camilla. Serenity and her growing family.

I park in front of the family garage and wave away the attendant before striding in through the side door of the house.

"*Mio figlio*, you're home," Mamma says from the kitchenette.

I stop to exchange kisses on the cheeks and accept her open scrutiny as any wise son would. After admonishing me for being away too long, she points me toward my father's study and warns me against keeping him waiting.

As I pass the dining room, I note the preparations for guests but pay little attention since my parents enjoy hosting small lunch parties often, but the somber air as I step into my father's study sends my brain into overdrive.

Knowing better than to skip the formalities with my father, I greet both him and my uncle before following their lead and joining them on the couches.

When my father splays his fingers over his armrest and squares his shoulders, I mentally brace myself while maintaining my attentive yet comfortable posture.

"There are rumors we need to dispel."

My heart lurches, but I blank my mind and relax my face. I haven't tried to keep my activities a secret from him, but I never asked his permission to go on a torturous rampage, either.

We should be beyond this. I'm not a child. He raised me to take over the family empire, and I've proven more than capable, yet he stunts my authority at every opportunity.

"We never expected Serenity to marry first. What happened to Camilla was horrible." Uncle Narciso rolls his glass between his fingers as he considers his next words. "But we salvaged the relationship between the Vivaldi and Russo families with your younger sister's wedding."

"It's only been two months since Serenity married, but we can't ignore the rumors when they're costing us business," my father says.

I quirk a brow despite the dread settling in my gut. This is not the topic I expected to discuss.

"Which rumors?" I ask.

"The ones about you being gay," my father says.

"Or infertile," Uncle Narciso sneers.

A muscle ticks in my father's jaw as he clenches his teeth in disgust. My mind refuses to grasp the ridiculousness of the conversation.

It's true I haven't visited our clubs recently, but anyone with half an ear to the ground would know it's because I've been busy elsewhere.

"You're getting married in four months. We expect a pregnancy announcement before the end of the first year."

I blink at my father. He must be joking, but his unwavering gaze tells me otherwise.

My parents always made it abundantly clear my marriage would never actually be mine, so the news doesn't shock me, but the timing fills me with unease.

I fix my suit coat and relax deeper into the couch as though I don't give a shit and meet his watchful eyes.

"Who am I marrying?"

"Aurora Achilles."

Disbelief runs down my spine. The last time I saw Aurora Achilles, she was an awkward and scrawny preteen. Dressed in a frilly white dress for an outdoor summer wedding, she'd pulled her brother away from me as though I had the plague, then fainted right at my feet. At nineteen, it was the most embarrassing moment of my life.

"How old is she?" I ask.

"Eighteen."

Something in my uncle's countenance splits my attention between him and the thoughts thundering through my mind.

If Aurora is eighteen now, then she's seven years younger than I am. She must have been about twelve years old when she fainted at my feet, so it's been over six years since I've seen her.

In fact, I've not heard anything about her since then either. No one has even said her name.

Her parents rarely miss social events, but they never mention her or her brother.

My unease grows.

"Why the long face, Giorgio?" my father asks.

When I meet the calculating gleam in his dark eyes, ice encases my soul.

"I haven't seen her in years. She was still a child the last time I saw her."

"Does it matter what she looks like now?" My uncle chuckles as he clinks the ice in his glass. "She's eighteen. I doubt you'll have trouble wedding and bedding her." He takes a sip and sets his glass down on the coffee table. "You're both in your prime. Just have some fun breaking her in and knocking her up, then go back to playing around at the club."

I grind my teeth and suck down a steadying breath before leaning forward and propping my elbows on my knees.

"She's an Achilles, *mio frio*. I'm not sure that's the best advice, but I'll keep it in mind."

His pupils shrink as I glare at him, daring him to refute me.

The Achilles family may not be as prominent as the Vivaldi family, but they have their own power. As one of New York City's founding mafia families, only the stupid would dare cross them.

My uncle isn't dumb. He wouldn't say something so insulting in public, but he shouldn't say it in private, either. Not after throwing unexpected news at me.

I sit back and sigh.

"Fine, then. A wedding in four months. When do we meet my bride-to-be?" I ask.

"Now. They should arrive any minute for lunch," my father says.

It's an underhanded tactic, and I don't appreciate him using it on me, but voicing my frustration won't help me now.

I aim unimpressed eyes at the man I once revered and allow more of my respect to fall away. With rage, guilt, and self-hatred fueling me, I see him as I've never seen him before.

Yes, he's a powerful, deadly man, but he's no longer the protector I once assumed he was.

We both failed my sisters, yet he shows no remorse.

"Good. Let's get this over with, then," I growl and wrap my determination to remain aloof in their presence around my spine.

It won't be difficult. All I have to think about is how humiliating it was to have a tiny, gangly mafia princess wrapped in frills pass out at my feet.

Until I step into the foyer and come face-to-face with a fallen angel. With emerald eyes, legs for days, and trim curves that would tempt a saint, Aurora Achilles may be the most gorgeous woman I've ever laid eyes on.

I'm so fucked.

CHAPTER 3

Aurora Achilles

MY MOTHER GLARES AT ME as my father exits the car and reaches for her door. Fear squeezes my heart.

I turn my attention to the ornate house outside my window. It gives me no clue who we're meeting, but in mere moments, I'll come face-to-face with the man who holds my future in his hands.

When the attendant opens my door, I accept his offered hand and step out of the vehicle but wait until my parents start up the stairs before trailing behind them.

The front door opens. Adrenaline floods my system. Apprehension adds extra weight to my feet. Dread coalesces in my chest as a vaguely familiar woman greets my parents. She ushers us into the foyer.

I meet dark chocolate eyes and freeze as mortification locks me in place. The blood drains from my face and pools in the pit of my stomach.

No. Not him. Anyone but him.

I stare into Giorgio Vivaldi's sinfully handsome face and wonder which god I pissed off.

He was unbearably good-looking at nineteen, but now, in his mid-twenties, he exudes sensual wickedness along with masculine power. I fight the urge to turn and run.

His lips flatten in disapproval. Pain streaks through my heart. I pull my shoulders back and step forward at my father's behest.

"Aurora, you remember Matteo and Bianca Vivaldi, right?" my mother asks. The change in her persona as she acts as the matron of the Achilles family makes me want to puke.

"Of course, Mamma. It's wonderful to see you again," I lie and accept Bianca Vivaldi's welcome. She gives me a half hug and kisses me on each cheek before holding me at arm's length.

"How long has it been since we've seen you? Five or six years? You've grown into a beauty, haven't you, Aurora?"

I offer her my best non-wooden smile and thank her for the compliment even though the hard edge to her expression relays her dissatisfaction. My stomach churns on the protein bar I forced myself to eat as I dressed, but I mentally pat myself on the back for not arriving on an empty stomach.

When my future mother-in-law passes me to her husband, I don't dare look over his shoulder at his son, nor do I seek help from my parents. I meet Matteo Vivaldi's eyes and study his expression as he studies me. My skin crawls as he gives a small smile and leans down to kiss the back of my hand.

"I must say, my son is a lucky man. Don't you think, Giorgio?"

In my attempt to avoid Giorgio Vivaldi's eyes as long as possible, I note the veiled threat within Matteo's tone and fight a fresh wave of nausea as his weathered face tightens in warning. He turns and offers my hand to Giorgio.

Fear and dismay turn to stone in my chest as my future husband quirks a sarcastic brow and takes my hand with exaggerated care.

"Of course."

His inflection says he most certainly does *not* feel lucky. I swallow the emotions clogging my throat and fight the urge to pull my hand away as he presses his lips to my knuckles.

Shock roots me to the spot as he sneaks his tongue between my fingers. The unexpectedly soft stroke steals my breath despite how fleeting and mocking it may be.

I lean on my mother's training and smile as though my face hasn't turned beet red.

"You're too kind. Truly," I say.

Despite my best efforts, my mother's glare relays my failure to hide my displeasure.

"Ah, Narciso, it's nice to see you. Will you be joining us for lunch?"

I stiffen at the delight in my father's voice and follow his gaze to the man emerging from the hall. I mask my instinctual cringe and attempt to free my hand from Giorgio's, but he tightens his fingers around mine.

"Unfortunately, no. I was just wrapping up some business with *mio fratello*, so I'm heading out and thought I'd introduce myself along the way."

Ants skitter along my flesh as he approaches, and for no reason other than a gut feeling, I'm thankful for Giorgio's grip on my hand.

"May I?" Narciso asks with a gesture toward our locked hands.

I struggle to breathe as tension fills the air. After a hair-raising moment, Giorgio responds.

"Maybe next time, *mio zio*. It is my first time seeing my bride-to-be in years, after all."

The amount of disdain packed into his words raises the hairs on my nape, but to my surprise, his uncle backs down.

"Next time, then. For now, it's nice to see you again, Aurora," he says.

His eyes trail up my body as he rises from his slight bow. Bile rises in my throat, but I offer him a polite smile.

As Narciso excuses himself and exits into the sunlight, I take a deep breath to calm myself, but Giorgio's woodsy cologne fills my nostrils. My heart skips a beat as my mouth waters and sensual thoughts streak through my mind.

"Let's continue this over lunch, shall we?" Matteo suggests. He takes Bianca by the arm and gestures for my parents to follow them.

My mother gives my father a hate-filled glance as he rests his fingertips on the back of her elbow, but she allows him to guide her down the hall after our hosts.

I flick my gaze up to Giorgio's face to gauge his reaction, but he's not watching my parents. With his gaze trained on the front door, he clenches his teeth together before filling his lungs and swinging his eyes to mine. He pierces my soul with his intense stare. The floor drops out from under my feet.

"You won't faint right in front of me again, will you?"

For an embarrassing moment, my brain relishes the sound of his voice instead of processing his words, but I suck down a steadying breath and swallow my jumbled emotions.

"It depends. Do you plan on starving me, or will you let me go so I can enjoy the meal your mother so graciously planned for us?"

He quirks his brow before shaking his head. "Neither."

I scoff at his curt response and try to pull away, but he yanks me toward him so hard I lose my balance. His massive hands close around my upper arms and stop me from crashing into him. For a horrible moment, disappointment streaks through me as his broad chest fills my vision. I want to know how it feels to press against his hard muscles. Common sense kicks in and my anger returns.

I stomp on his foot and shove my fists into his rock hard, unforgiving abs and wince as pain pulses through my knuckles. He snarls and tightens his grip on my arms without giving an inch.

"Really, Aurora? This is what we're doing?"

Tears of frustration burn my eyes, so I tuck my chin to my chest and pray my hair hides my face.

I can't breathe. My lungs ache.

This wasn't at all what I expected from today. Ever since my mother sprung the news on me this morning, I promised myself I'd make it through the day without an ounce of emotion. I would hide behind a mask of indifference and then cry after she locked my door tonight.

I could have done it, too, if it had been any other man besides Giorgio Vivaldi, but it wasn't.

The moment I saw his chiseled face, my mask crumbled and unwanted memories flooded me. It's too much.

"But then again, why should I expect anything less from a spoiled little girl who passed out at my feet in the middle of a packed wedding reception?"

His mocking words help me gather and weld together the pieces of my broken mask. I suck down a ragged breath and fight against his hold.

"Just let me go," I half plead, half demand through gritted teeth.

"No. I'm a man of my word, *mia topolina*, and I don't enjoy repeating myself, so make it easier on yourself and stop fighting me," he rumbles in a voice I shouldn't find sexy, but the deep vibrations travel straight to my core.

I squeak as he pivots and tucks me against his side. His heavy hand settles on my waist as his massive body dwarfs mine.

Every nerve in my body sparks to life as awareness spears through me. He could crush me without even trying. I feel tiny and vulnerable pressed against him. Our size difference astounds me.

Then his words sink in through my lust, and indignant fury wells up from my depths.

"*Mia topolina?*" I scoff and elbow his side, but bite back a hiss when I realize I might as well be hitting granite. "I'm not a mouse, and I'm definitely not yours, so don't call me that."

His only response is a noncommittal hum and a tightening of his fingers around my waist. He starts forward, and with reluctant steps, I follow his lead. Halfway down the hall, I realize he was telling the truth.

He neither plans to starve nor release me.

With a few demeaning words and even less effort, this jerk stole my sense of control and proved his dominance over me.

I struggle against rising hopelessness as my future spans out in front of me. Years of uncertainty and subjugation under yet another tyrannical ruler like my mother fill my thoughts with dark, lonely clouds, but I push them away and focus on what's most important.

I'll agree to anything—*anything*—if it keeps Tristan safe just a little longer. I'm so close to having everything we need to escape this horrible life, but if the time comes and I can't stay under my parents' roof to protect him, I'll have to send my brother off on his own.

Nothing matters beyond protecting Tristan.

Not even this wickedly handsome, frustratingly brusque, tatted mafia prince who once saw me at my lowest and seems keen to hold it against me.

Despite my body's reaction to his as he hauls me down the hall, I build a mental barrier between us and remind myself why we're here.

Our parents wait in the dining room. They'll ultimately plan every aspect of our lives until the day of our wedding, and even after then, their stipulations will no doubt rule our decisions.

My heart skips a beat as Giorgio flexes his fingers into my waist and pulls me tighter against his side.

What wouldn't I do to have his strength? His powerful physique? His authority?

If it weren't for his rudeness, I may have reacted better and made him an ally instead of a foe, but that code crumbled along with my preteen body when I fainted in front of him, so the *let's-be-friends* program crashed and burned before I could even start laying the foundation.

I push down my frustration and focus on the trials ahead.

I'll do whatever it takes to keep my brother safe, even if it means going toe-to-toe with Giorgio Vivaldi.

CHAPTER 4

Giorgio Vivaldi

AURORA ACHILLES FITS PERFECTLY against my side. I long to feel her bare flesh pressed against mine as I watch her emerald eyes widen in shock and lower in delight as I build her pleasure to new heights. Visions of her naked and writhing in my sheets have me half hard in my trousers.

Which isn't a good impression as I turn us into the dining room.

The calculating expressions on every face in the room clear away the heat simmering in my blood.

But maybe my lust isn't such a bad thing. Showing my interest in her may buy me more time to find the culprit behind the attacks on my family. If my parents believe an heir is inevitable—and soon—they might loosen their grip on my immediate future and grant me the freedom to continue my mission.

I tease my fingertips along Aurora's ribs and enjoy her startled inhale as my thumb brushes against the lower swell of her breast.

God, I want to explore every inch of her, tasting and teasing her from head to toe. I bet my hand would dwarf her pert little breast as her hard nipple pressed against my palm.

"I knew they'd be a perfect match," my mother says in a conspiratorial stage whisper to Aurora's mother.

Madona Achilles studies us with haughty eyes before smiling and leaning forward to respond to my mother.

"They're getting along quite well, aren't they? I'm sure we're all quite pleased."

I eye the places readied at the table and decide to play by my mother's rules for the time being. I'd much rather have Aurora sitting beside me where I can touch her whenever I want, but with the upcoming conversation, I want her face in clear view so I can study her expressions.

She hesitates when I start around the table, but I don't give her a choice to balk. Her stiff shoulders annoy the hell out of me, but they remind me of what's at stake.

The soft sway of her hips teases me as nothing else ever has before.

I'll enjoy breaking down her walls and molding her to my will. For now, I'll focus on learning as much as I can about her.

When I remove my arm from around her and pull out her chair, she aims skeptical eyes up at me. I sigh and guide her into her seat with a loose grip on her elbow.

Her prim and proper pose as she perches on the edge of her seat awakens the beast within me. Feral hunger grips me as I imagine wrecking her with my teeth and tongue, so I scoot her chair closer to the table, appeasing the monster within me by ruining her faux propriety.

She grunts and grips the edge of the table as I force her deeper into the seat. Once I'm satisfied she's suitably riled, I smirk down at her and stride around the table to my seat.

The blush on her cheeks highlights her doll-like features, but as our parents feel each other out with small talk, her face pales.

I keep my eyes focused solely on her as the kitchen staff brings out the first wave of dishes.

"Since they both seem eager, I have no problem with a quicker timeline. We don't need a year to prepare a wedding," Horatio Achilles, Aurora's father, says.

My father nods and picks up his glass.

"I agree, the sooner the better, but we don't want more rumors," he says.

The fake concern marring his brows as he studies his drink sends ice down my spine.

"Maybe we do."

Everyone swivels their attention to Madona as her words register.

"What do you mean?" my mother asks.

The ice infecting my spine spreads to my limbs as my mother's deceit registers. I take a sip of water to hide my anger. She knew before she greeted me today what news awaited me. In fact, she planned how to direct this entire conversation with my father. She knew it would come to this, yet didn't say a word to me.

"Aurora is eighteen. She's an Achilles. There's nothing wrong with her being so madly in love with Giorgio Vivaldi she has a shotgun wedding," Madona Achilles says.

To my surprise, Aurora lifts her fork to her mouth and slips a bite between her lips as though the words don't affect her at all. She keeps her gaze trained on her plate, but the tightness around her eyes and her reluctance to swallow speak volumes.

She's fully aware of the conversation and definitely opposes, but the little mouse remains quiet even as her mother throws her to the wolves.

My mother counteracts with faux concern.

"We couldn't do that to Aurora; plus, we shouldn't risk your family name for the sake of ours."

"Oh, please, it won't bother Aurora at all. She's never listened to gossip anyway, and we're not risking anything. We're honored to associate with the Vivaldi's," Madona says.

"You're too kind," my mother responds.

Madona dabs her painted lips with her napkin and folds it back into her lap as though she's royalty before speaking.

"I'm not being kind. We want what's best for both families. If that means pregnancy before a wedding, then we should explore our options."

For the briefest of moments, Aurora's features twist, but she closes her eyes and inhales through her nose before blanking her expression and putting food on her fork as though there's nothing amiss.

I trace the base of my glass with one finger, playing in the condensation, and curl my other hand into a fist under the table.

The entire conversation between our mothers is too absurd. Not a single word spoken is believable. The more I hear, the less inclined I am to trust our parental units.

And I don't like the pain shining from Aurora's eyes. Her anguish was beautiful when I was the one wielding it, but sourness coats my tongue as I watch her suffer under someone else's verbal blows.

She hides it better than most, but there's no denying the slow death of her soul as her mother chips away at her dignity. I've watched countless men breathe their last, but no one has affected me the way her haunted eyes do.

I miss the spark of defiance as she glared at me.

Fuck, I'm so screwed. I'm obsessed after only a few minutes with her.

"Other than a few college courses—which she can always retake at a later date—she has no other commitments."

Her mother's words pull me out of my musings, and I realize I missed part of their conversation.

Aurora's fingers tighten around her fork and her nostrils flare, but she sits with her back rigid and her mouth shut.

As fresh fury sparkles in her eyes, I long to have those gorgeous, fiery green orbs aimed at me.

"But we can only rush a wedding so much. Our children deserve a proper ceremony," my mother says.

"I agree, but there are other factors to consider, too. Six months would be too long. If she gets pregnant right away, she'll be showing too much, but if she doesn't, then worse rumors will spread about our families' power."

"Four months might be manageable," my mother delivers flawlessly.

Aurora's hand shakes as she brings the fork to her lips again, but she sticks the tiny bite into her mouth and chews with striking determination.

"They should move in together as soon as possible," Madona says.

Aurora freezes. Blinks. Clenches her jaw. Blinks again. The tears shimmering in her eyes both enrage and enchant me.

"Since Aurora has nothing tying her to one place, why don't we—"

I watch in fascination as Aurora's composure snaps. She slaps her fork onto the table, spits her mouthful into her napkin, and tosses it onto her plate as she stands.

She glares at her mother. In mere seconds, she conveys more emotions than I can count, so when she shifts her gaze toward her father and sends a fresh wave to him, all I can do is stare in awe.

Without a word or a backward glance, she leaves the room.

I follow before her mother breaks the silence, far more interested in my little mouse than in the farce between our parents.

With an uncanny sense of direction, Aurora reaches the guest bathroom before I catch up with her, but I wedge my foot between the door and the frame before she can close it behind her.

My balls ache as she lifts shimmering green orbs up to my face. Her deep, even inhale through her nose only heightens my desire.

"Please remove your foot from the door," she says in a harsh and forceful voice.

She vibrates with fury. I want to see her break. I need to see her wild, raw, and exposed.

"No. Let me in, *mia topolina*," I growl.

"Don't mock me! I just..." She pushes against the door. Desperation creeps into her tone. "I just need a minute alone."

"Move away from the door, Aurora. I don't want to hurt you."

"Then go away! Please, Giorgio, I—"

The sound of my name on her lips shreds my control. I push my way into the bathroom and lock the door behind me.

She squeaks and shuffles backward. I crowd her against the wall and lean down when she averts her gaze, but not before I enjoy the widening of her eyes and the flush of her cheeks.

Her chest heaves with her startled breaths, and I resist the urge to plaster my front against hers by bracing my forearms on the wall, bracketing her in without touching her.

She's so feminine and petite. I ache with the need to make her mine.

"Don't say my name unless you want me all over you. Understand, little mouse?"

"No, I don't. I do *not* understand."

HEARTLESS VOWS

Tempting my demons, I tilt her chin up with my knuckle before propping my forearm back on the wall.

"What don't you understand?"

"Why are you doing this?"

"Because you're mine, Aurora."

As I say the words, certainty barrels through me. She became mine the moment she walked through my parents' front door. Nothing our families say matters. Whether we marry today, tomorrow, in four months, or four years, it does not fucking matter.

Aurora Achilles is mine.

She scoffs and shakes her head.

"That doesn't explain why you're being a complete jerk. Isn't this situation bad enough already?"

I growl, pinch her chin between my thumb and forefinger, and force her eyes to mine.

"Excuse me?" I challenge.

She swallows and defiantly fans her lashes against her cheeks for a few seconds before meeting my stare and speaking slowly, as though to an invalid.

"You. Are. Being. A. Jerk."

I stare in shock long after her words register, but her expression doesn't change.

I expected her to elaborate on why the situation was terrible, not to call me out with such unwavering boldness.

My hand moves without my permission, but I savor the pounding of her pulse as I wrap my fingers around her throat.

"Say that again," I dare.

Her lower lip trembles, but she squares her shoulders and maintains eye contact as she responds.

"I'm a woman of my word, and I don't like to repeat myself, so why don't you make it easy on both of us and. Stop. Being. A. Jerk."

No one in my adult life, except for possibly Fiero, has ever spoken to me with such snark. No one else would have survived the consequences.

But this tiny slip of a woman stands her ground and uses my own words against me.

I'm enamored. Hooked. Delighted.

Doomed.

I flick my gaze down to her lush lips before I lower my mouth a hairsbreadth away from hers.

"You want me to stop, but I haven't even begun, have I, *mia topolina?*"

She closes her eyes and tries to turn her face away, but I tighten my grip on her throat and sneak my tongue along the bottom edge of her lower lip.

"Do you really want me to stop, Aurora?"

Her choppy breaths warm my lips, but her low, throaty *please* destroys my control.

"Just one taste. I just need one taste, then I'll stop," I lie before closing the distance between our lips.

I hum in delight at her softness and brush my closed mouth back and forth across hers before dipping my tongue between her lips. Her clenched teeth prevent me from exploring her depths, but I need more, so I flex my fingers around her throat and take advantage when she gasps.

The hot sweetness of her mouth overrides the rest of world and becomes my new favorite addiction, and when I stroke my tongue over hers, I groan from the force of my need.

She pushes at my sides and trembles, so close to giving in, but she maintains her defiance despite the hammering of her throat against my palm and the pebbling of her nipples against my chest. I pull back and feast my eyes on her flushed face and swollen lips.

"This is the opposite of not being a jerk," she deadpans with her chin raised and her eyes closed.

Her tiny fingers dig into my sides. She trembles from head to toe.

I'm an idiot for wanting her, but I can't pull away now. Not after I've had a taste.

Aurora Achilles may be the death of me, but I'll protect her no matter what it takes.

No one will hurt her except for me, and when I do, she'll beg for more.

So much more.

CHAPTER 5

Aurora Achilles

FIRE ROARS THROUGH MY VEINS and yearning spears through my soul, but I replay my mother's threat from this morning in my mind and wait until the worst of the storm subsides. I can't leave Tristan all alone in that fucked up household.

I open my eyes. My heart leaps as a muscle ticks along Giorgio's jaw. Expecting to find him glaring at me, I blink in surprise and confusion at the softness in his gaze.

He drops his forehead to the wall beside my ear, surrounding me with his bulk and ghosting his breath over my sensitive skin, but when I shiver, he loosens his grip on my throat.

Heat pools low in my belly. As terrifying as it is to have his hand encasing my throat, I like the way it feels, and I know I should hate it, but an odd sense of security flows through me.

"I should apologize, but I don't think I can," he murmurs *oh so close* to my ear.

I scoff.

"What, are you going to excuse your horrible behavior like a high school bully? Aren't you too old for that? I didn't even go to high school, and I—"

He flexes his fingertips into my jugular, so I stop my nervous tirade.

"I thought you graduated. What do you mean you didn't go to high school?"

I swallow and stumble through my explanation.

"I was homeschooled. Well, online learning. At home. In fact, I rarely leave my house. I-I need my routine. I'm not against marrying you, truly. I just want to stay home until after our wedding. Give me some time to adjust to the change."

When he doesn't immediately refute me, I hold my breath against the hope rising in my chest.

He relaxes his fingers against my throat and brushes the pad of his thumb along my jawline. Shivers travel down my spine at the unexpectedly gentle and intimate caress.

"Do you want to marry me?"

I stiffen at his loaded question.

"I didn't know I was getting married until this morning," I answer.

His low chuckle arrows straight to my core.

"You knew before I did, then. My father ambushed me a few minutes before you arrived."

Shock filters through me at his wry honesty. My tongue loosens.

"I didn't know it was you I was marrying until I walked through your front door," I say.

For some ungodly reason, I can't stop challenging him at every turn.

"You win this round by a handful of minutes, then. I half expected a scrawny little kid covered in frills to stomp into the foyer. Maybe that's why I can't keep my hands off you. You're too fucking gorgeous, *mia topolina*."

Electricity buzzes through me as he skims his nose over the shell of my ear and traces his thumb higher on my chin, barely teasing my bottom lip. I push against his chest and tilt my face away from him.

He growls and nips my ear in displeasure. I gasp at the delicious sting and struggle to comprehend his words as he speaks.

"You said you were okay with this. Why are you shying away?"

I take a shuddering breath and swallow before responding.

"It's just so sudden. Please, Gio—" I stop myself from saying his name as his warning rings in my ears. "Please don't yank me away from the only constant I've ever had in my life. Let me live at my home until our wedding."

"Why would I do that? Why would I limit my access to you when I could have you naked in my bed twenty-four seven?"

The guttural quality of his voice as he nuzzles my temple and teases my neck, ear, and face with his fingers sends throbbing interest through my belly.

"If I can have dinner and breakfast with my family and sleep in my room at night, I'll do anything you want."

"Anything?"

Only an idiot would miss the dirty suggestion in his tone. I dig my knuckles into his rock-hard muscles and ignore the desperation filling my voice.

"Yes."

"Prove it," he whispers against my ear.

Tendrils of dread sneak through my chest, but I firm my resolve and remind myself nothing is too drastic if it means protecting my brother.

"How do I prove it?" I ask, even though I already know what he'll say.

"Kiss me."

I pause, taken aback by his answer. I expected something much lewder, especially since he already stole a kiss from me.

"Okay, I can do that," I say before I try to think my way out of it.

"A real kiss, Aurora. Not some hesitant, teenage fumbling, but a deep and dirty kiss to prove how much you want me. Make me hungry. Make me hard. Make me desperate for you."

He licks the shell of my ear. I bite back a groan and press harder against the wall.

Part of me wants him hotter and hungrier than he is now, but I'm already overwhelmed by his attention, so I'm not sure I'd survive more.

I can't fail my brother, and there's no point in denying Giorgio since our parents insist we marry, so I push aside my misgivings and open my hands to press my palms against his chest.

"Okay. I'll do it. I'll kiss you."

Even to my own ears, I sound like I'm giving myself a pep talk. He lifts his head and pins me in place with the intensity of his gaze.

For long, endless moments, I drown in the depths of his eyes. Almost dark enough to appear black, his irises hide a rich brown hue.

He's going to eat me alive. An inferno rages in my core. I skim my hands up to his shoulders—his strong, impossibly wide shoulders—and fight an entire flock of butterflies as his attention dips to my lips. He pushes my chin up with his thumb and spans his thick fingers around my neck.

I dig my nails into his shoulders and lock my muscles, halting his descent, and search his expression.

"Wait. I know you don't have the final say, but if I do this, you promise you'll help me? Promise you'll fight for me, even if it means going against both of our parents?"

My ribs ache as I hold my breath, waiting for his answer.

It would be so easy for him to lie to me—or just take what he wants—but no matter how cruel or demeaning he's been, I can't help but trust him.

First impressions leave a mark. He may not remember, but our reunion in the foyer wasn't the start of our relationship, and neither was the mortifying incident six years ago when I fainted at his feet.

His low, animalistic rumble turns my bones to mush.

"I'd fight the world if you asked me to, so just give me a goddamn kiss already."

It's the most ridiculous thing I've ever heard, but my heart flutters and heat pulses between my legs. I pull him down to me before I lose my nerve.

He eagerly bends down but stops with his lips a millimeter away from mine. I close my eyes, rise onto tiptoes, and press our lips together, praying I don't fuck up what could be my only chance to earn Giorgio Vivaldi as an ally.

When he doesn't open his mouth or further the kiss, panic grips my heart, but the softness of his lips enchants me. It's fascinating how such a tall, dark, and lethal man could have even an ounce of softness on his impressive body. Even if it's only his lips, my curiosity wins, and the lump of embarrassment and fear lodged in my chest dissipates as I explore him.

His hot breath warms my face as I brush my lips over his.

It's not enough.

I test his bottom lip with my tongue. When he doesn't take over, I lose myself in cataloguing every centimeter of his lips, teeth, and tongue, until urgency sweeps me away and I can no longer discern where I end and he begins.

Every cell in my body animates. Need throbs in my clit. My nipples harden. Wetness dampens my panties.

He pulls back. I chase him. He tightens his grip on my throat and stops me.

Reality crashes down on my head. I shake from head to toe, but I can't unsheathe my nails from his nape.

I don't know when I released his shoulders and started clawing at the back of his neck, but his heavy-lidded gaze tells me he doesn't mind. In fact, his lopsided smirk encourages me to do it harder. To scratch him deeper. To leave my mark on him.

Despite my death grip on him, he doesn't press his body to mine.

Did I do something wrong? Am I reading too much into his expression? Is he mocking me again?

"You're fucking delicious, *mia topolina*. More. Again."

I tuck my face against my arm mere milliseconds before his mouth crashes onto mine.

"I-I did what you asked. I kissed you. You promised."

He groans and drops his forehead to my temple.

"I did. I will. I'll fight for you, Aurora."

Weight lifts from my shoulders and I sag against the wall. My shoulders and neck ache from the odd angle, but I don't dare let go of his nape.

My reprieve doesn't last.

He flicks the tip of his tongue over my cheekbone in a teasing lick before dropping his mouth to my jawline and brushing his lips over my flesh as he speaks. His half whisper, half growl travels down my chest and throbs in my nipples.

"But I never said I'd stop touching you. I'll protect and ravage you at the same time."

I twist my fingernails deeper into his nape and whimper as he nips and licks his way down the side of my throat.

"No, wait. You can't."

"I can and I w—"

We both startle as I slap my palm over his mouth, and for an absurd moment, I wonder who moved my body without my permission. My heart pounds in my throat. I swallow and consider peeling my hand off his face but decide to trust my knee jerk reaction.

"Don't say it. Man of your word, remember?"

After a terrifying moment, the cold fury in his gaze fades away, so I rush to explain.

"You can't protect me if you knock me up without legal ties already in place."

He quirks a brow.

"No matter what our parents say, their verbal agreements won't hold up in a court of law."

His eyes darken. I press my palm harder against his mouth and continue.

"I know, I know, in this lifestyle, a man's word is supposed to be law, but... I don't trust them. I know it sounds stupid, but we should sign a prenuptial agreement before—"

He removes his forearm from the wall for the first time in forever and pulls my hand away from his mouth. His thick fingers cover most of my forearm as he holds my wrist.

"Is this part of some elaborate, convoluted scheme? Did your mother put you up to this?"

I suffer a keen sense of abandonment as he rises to his full height, forcing me to release his nape, but his fingers still wrapped around my throat keep me grounded.

"No! I don't know what my parents are thinking, which is why I don't trust them," I say.

When his skepticism doesn't wane, I swallow and touch the wrist near my throat. He flexes before loosening his grip and sliding his hand to my collarbone, pinning me back against the wall. With my other arm trapped in his and held above my shoulder, a wave of powerlessness washes over me, but I firm my resolve.

My brother's safety and future are more important.

"I don't want your money. I want your protection."

The hard edge leaves his expression.

"The prenuptial would be for *us*. To protect you and me against whatever our parents hope to gain from our union."

Funny sensations flutter through my belly as he sharpens his attention to my eyes.

"Write whatever conditions you want in the agreement. I don't care, as long as we're both legally protected if things go sideways…" I decide to take a chance and include my next thought, even if it means his fury returns. "Which includes protection from each other."

After a few tense moments, he quirks his brow and lifts his arm, forcing me onto my tiptoes.

"Is this a warning in disguise, Aurora?" Before I can respond, he yanks my hand to his nape, pulling me off the wall and flush against his front as he wraps his other arm around my waist and rests his hand on my lower back. "Because if you're trying to scare me away, it won't work." He leans forward until his lips brush against my ear, bending me backward and grinding our bodies together. "I like the way you challenge me as you sink your nails into my flesh.

I'm already addicted, *mia topolina*." Magma bubbles in my core as he curls his tongue over the shell of my ear. "No one can protect you from me, but I'm also the only one allowed to hurt you from now on." I bite back a groan as he nips the top of my earlobe. "*Capisci?*"

It's too much. *He's* too much.

"Yes. I understand," I say in a breathy voice.

"Good girl. Now give me another kiss to tie me over until after lunch."

"After lunch?"

"We're signing a prenup as soon as possible. I'm not waiting a second longer than necessary to have you. You're mine, Aurora."

I should hate his declaration of ownership. I'm not an object.

My body doesn't listen.

In less than an hour, Giorgio Vivaldi barged his way into my life and completely rewrote my body's framework, and now my brain struggles to process the new set of rules.

I'm so fucking screwed.

CHAPTER 6

Giorgio Vivaldi

SHE'S PUTTY IN MY HANDS. Soft, vulnerable, and so fucking perfect, I've got the worst case of blue balls. One kiss isn't enough.

She's mine. I need her. Now.

I lean down to take her lips, not waiting for her reply, and growl when she tucks her face against my chest.

"Are you sure you can stop?"

With her forehead tucked against my sternum, one hand gripping my lapel, and her other wrist trapped in my grip near my shoulder, she rules my world, filling me with carnal hunger, but the uncertainty in her tone makes me pause.

Her innocence shines through the question. Even though she acts tough, her reaction to every touch assures me she's never done this before. I need all her firsts.

I growl and tighten my arm around her.

"You can run and hide all you like, Aurora. Nothing will stop me from taking what I want, and what I want is *you*."

"I'm not trying to deny you. If you say you can stop before you go too far, then I'll trust you. Man of your word, remember?"

She trembles from head to toe as she speaks, but with her face hidden in my chest, I can't read her expression to know if it's from fear or desire or both.

It doesn't matter, not when she's placed her trust in me despite how I haven't earned it.

I release her wrist and drop my head back, telling myself to let her go, but I wrap my other arm around her and cover most of her back with my hands. She's petite, delicate, and soft—the opposite of my hard, masculine body. Her curves fit so perfectly against mine, liquid fire surges down my shaft and escapes from my tip. I grind my teeth and stare at the ceiling, willing my cock to quit testing my trouser seams and ignoring the wet spot forming on the fabric.

"No, I'm not sure I'll stop, but I can't let you go yet, either, *mia topolina*. I need more."

"How much more?"

She's right to be wary, but I don't like the trepidation in her tone, so I peel one arm off her and brace my palm on the wall. Her fingers tighten on my lapels.

"Don't move," I snarl.

She barely breathes as I fight against the urge to pin her up against the wall and take what I want, but the rapid pounding of her heart alerts my predatory instincts to the prey trapped in my arms. It would be so easy to flip up her skirt, wrap her legs around my hips, and surge balls deep into her tight, wet heat.

"If I touch you, I'm taking everything, but this is as much *stopping* as I can handle," I growl.

She swallows but remains stiff and unmoving against me. I lower my head and meet her bright green eyes.

"So… you want me to touch you? Is that where this is going?"

Her intelligence is sexy as hell. Despite the incredulity in her tone and her attempt at sounding angry, the flush on her cheeks and dazed look in her eyes reveal her interest.

My cock throbs in demand, but I grit my teeth and say what I must.

"Tell me you don't want to, and I'll walk away, but only this once, and I won't hold back next time I get you alone. There'll be no negotiating. No gentleness. Just hot, raw sex. Is that what you want, *mia topolina?*"

Her inhale shifts her breasts against my stomach. My fingers itch to explore.

"No. That's not what I want, but…"

Need pulses at the base of my spine.

"But?" I prod.

"I've never done *any* of… this," she says with the most appealing blush darkening her cheeks.

Molten lava escapes my balls and sears the inside of my shaft. I suck down a steadying breath and dig my fingers into her lower back.

"You've never touched a man?" I ask.

"Never," she says while shaking her head.

I tilt my hips and enjoy her gasp as my hard cock grinds against her soft belly.

"Have you ever been touched by a man?"

The jealousy flashing through me at the thought of anyone else pleasuring her nearly blinds me, but she shakes her head and clings to my vest.

"How has such a tempting *topolina* like you remained so pure for eighteen goddamn years?" I groan.

She stiffens and looks away to hide her thoughts, but I growl and dip my fingers to the upper swell of her ass. Her startled emerald orbs become the center of my universe.

"Are you lying to me, Aurora? Is this innocence an act?"

"It's not! I gave you my first kiss, and now you're back to being an ass. Let me go."

I growl and fill my hand with her ass. She gasps and tugs at my lapels as I shift her higher up my body.

"Is that what you really want? Do you want me to walk away and come back half mad from wanting you? Want me wild and desperate? Want your first time to be fast and rough?"

The tears shimmering in her eyes are the only thing keeping me from ravaging her.

"You're mocking me," she accuses.

"I'm not. I'm torturing myself. Decide now, Aurora, before I lose control."

I watch in a daze of lust as she pulls her anger around her like a shield. With a mix of impertinence and uncertainty, she seals her fate.

"Don't walk away," she demands.

"Then touch me," I growl.

Her eyes search my face.

"Can you put both hands on the wall?" she asks.

I try—I really do—but her ass fits so perfectly in my palm, I can't.

"No."

She broke me down to single syllable answers and animalistic snarls with just the promise of her hands on me.

She pries her hands off my lapels before going straight to my belt.

I underestimated her. She knows exactly how to render me speechless.

I snarl, release her ass, and yank her head back by her hair. She hisses in pain but unfastens my trousers without even looking.

"What, no foreplay? I thought this was all new to you," I manage through gritted teeth.

Her dainty hands shove my trousers off my hips and reach for the waistline of my boxer briefs.

"This is the root of the problem, isn't it? Why waste time when we both know this is what you meant?"

I twist my hand in her hair and nip her chin.

"Are you sure you know what you're doing, *mia topolina?*"

She scoffs.

"I've spent most of my life on the computer. I know what porn is."

She hisses when I pull her head back even further.

"Porn is child's play compared to what I want to do to you and watching is not experiencing, so think carefully before you stick your hand in my pants, Aurora. Do you really think you can handle this?"

"Well, you aren't giving me much choice, are you?"

Inexplicable joy blooms in my heart at the fire in her eyes. I much prefer the fury shimmering in her emerald orbs over the quiet pain as she endured her mother's insults at the table.

She pulls my waistband away from my body and reaches into my boxer briefs. I groan as her delicate fingers wrap around my shaft. The shock of her cool digits around my hard, pulsing cock nearly pushes me over the edge.

Liquid fire leaks from my tip.

The startled widening of her eyes as she tests my girth fills me with pride. When several seconds tick by and her hand remains in the same place, I groan and tangle my hand deeper into her hair.

"I thought you knew what you were doing?" I challenge, too close to losing control to dampen my antagonistic tone.

"I thought so, too," she whispers.

When she jolts and blushes, I realize she didn't mean to speak her thoughts out loud.

"Touch me, Aurora."

"I *am*. Give me a second. I didn't expect you to be so…"

I smirk and fight the urge to take her mouth, knowing I won't stop at one taste.

"So big?" I prod.

Several emotions flit across her features as she blinks at me. My chest tightens as she shakes her head.

"No. You're big everywhere, so I expected the size, but you're so…" she flexes her hand around me and shifts toward my tip, "warm and…" her honesty and gentle exploration will be the death of me, "silky?"

My cock hardens impossibly further and pulses in her hand. Her breath stutters and pupils dilate. She tries to glance down, but her gaze on mine is the only thing preventing me from losing control, so I twist my fingers in her hair and struggle to breathe as she explores my tip with barely there pressure.

"You're so soft," she murmurs.

My thighs tremble as she lightly strokes down my shaft. I curl my fingers against the wall, uncaring when the fancy paint chips under my nails.

"But so hard," she whispers.

It's too much. No matter how much I want to enjoy her as she explores me, the pressure at the base of my spine warns of my imminent eruption.

"Stop teasing and stroke me like you mean it," I growl.

She tucks her bottom lip between her teeth before tightening her grip around me.

I snarl and tilt her head to the side, stretching and exposing her throat so I can enjoy the thrumming of her pulse as she strokes me from base to tip.

"Get on your knees, *mia topolina*, and take my cock into your mouth."

I tug her hair. After a moment of hesitation, she sinks to her knees. I shuffle my feet apart to make room for her but keep one hand in her hair and the other against the wall. The wise little minx keeps her eyes on my face even as she works my underwear down enough to pull out my cock.

When I tilt my hips in demand, she leans back.

"Wait, I—"

She clamps her mouth shut when I crowd her closer to the wall and rub the underside of my cock against her face. Her fingers tighten around my base. My balls throb.

I hiss as she shifts her grip and angles my shaft away from her warm, smooth flesh.

"Not on my face. Or in my hair. I know some men like—"

Her words end on a hiss of pain as I yank her hair.

"You're going to swallow every drop, or we'll start over," I say.

Her pupils shrink, and for a moment, she looks mad enough to rebel, but she takes a deep breath and changes her grip so her nails rest against my sensitive flesh.

"No. I'm not some pet you can boss around, and just because I asked for your help doesn't make me a doormat." She steals chunks of my heart with her spunk and threatens my composure as her breath ghosts over my groin. "We're building our relationship around having a baby, so this is a onetime thing."

Her vehemence fills me with equal parts adoration and frustration.

"Don't test me, little girl. Open your mouth."

Fear clouds her eyes. Even as self-hatred curls in my gut, lust pools between my legs. She doesn't speak, but I loosen my fist and cup her head, giving her more freedom while protecting her skull from the wall.

After a flash of apprehension and gratitude, defiance fills her expression. She guides my cock back toward her face but doesn't open her mouth.

HEARTLESS VOWS

Trapped in the deepest, darkest layer of hell where pleasure becomes pain and pain becomes euphoria, I grit my teeth as she rubs my tip over her soft lips. After a few passes, she sneaks her tongue out and licks my slit.

I groan and draw tiny circles on her scalp. Her eyes soften.

My world shrinks to her eyes and mouth as she wraps her lips around my tip. With an adorable and stunning mix of surprise, interest, and hesitancy, she explores me from top to bottom, only keeping me in her mouth for half a second before licking down the underside of my shaft and trailing her tongue over my veins.

When she closes her lips around my tip again, I lose control and wrap both hands around her head. She squeaks and stacks her fists over my shaft, wisely preventing me from shoving deep into her throat.

She glares at me. I run my thumbs over her temples and brows, coaxing her to relax and apologizing without words. She tries to pull back, but I squeeze her head and flex my hips.

"If it's just this once, then give me what I want. Drop your hands."

She shakes her head. I smirk.

"So we'll be doing this again?"

After a moment of consideration, she moves her top hand to my thigh and quirks a challenge-filled brow at me.

Down on her knees with my cock in her mouth in one of the most submissive positions possible, the tiny, sassy mafia princess proves more resilient and powerful than anyone else I've ever met in my life. With a curl of her tongue, she does what dozens of people have tried to do but failed.

She wrecks the last of my control.

I piston in and out of her tight, wet mouth, hitting the back of her throat but unable to reach further with her hand clamped around my shaft.

It doesn't matter. With her emerald eyes locked on mine, I erupt faster and harder than I have since I was a young teen first exploring my body.

After a gagged sound of surprise, she swallows and stops fighting my grip on her head, but she flexes her fingers around my base and digs her nails into my thigh. For long, delirious moments, I enjoy the rush of release as I empty my balls into the tight grip of her mouth, and when my senses settle into reality, I gentle my hands in her hair and pet her with the reverence I don't have words for.

A tear escapes her lashes and trails down her cheek. My heart lurches in my chest, solidifying my demise.

Aurora Achilles owns my soul. She's more important than my sisters. More important than my parents.

Without her, I'm nothing.

I need her. All of her.

Now.

CHAPTER 7

Aurora Achilles

I FIGHT TO HOLD BACK MY TEARS as adrenaline and uncertainty spear through me, but lose the battle when he smears the single escaped tear from my cheek with his thumb. If he were to continue his domineering assholery, I could pull myself back together and save the emotions for later, but the pleasure and concern etched into his features break me.

One moment, I'm on my knees with his massive cock in my mouth, and the next, I'm pressed against his chest with his arms wrapped around me.

Too overwhelmed by the day's unexpected events, I sob harder than I have in years, uncertain what pushed me over the edge, but too far out of my comfort zone to rein my emotions back in.

His massive arms create a safe, comfortable place to fall apart, but when I realize my tears soak his expensive suit, I huff in exasperation and pull myself back together with thoughts of protecting my brother.

I tell myself I'm not dirty. Giorgio Vivaldi is my future husband, and he was surprisingly gentle and patient with me.

But I never thought my first sexual interaction would be so… intense yet one-sided. And in a bathroom, of all places. I never expected to feel so empowered despite how powerless I'd been on my knees.

And it's all because of him. Giorgio Vivaldi. He wasn't cruel or unyielding. In fact, his taunting helped me feel more in control.

And now he holds me in his arms like he cherishes me. It's too much.

I need him as an ally, but I can't lose sight of what's at stake by allowing my emotions to interfere, so I swallow the lump in my throat—enjoying the residual salty tang of his release—and wipe my tears away with the back of my hands.

"I'm okay. You can let me go now," I say.

"In a minute."

His curt response raises my hackles.

"No. Now."

He sighs and strokes his fingers through my hair.

"You may be okay, but I'm not. Be still, *mia topolina*, and let me hold you while I recover."

His admission shouldn't fill me with pride, but it does, so I lean my forehead on his hard chest and focus on regulating my breathing. The feel of his semi-hard cock against my stomach fills me with perverse interest and an unexpected sense of intimacy.

When he weaves his fingers into my hair and tugs my face up to meet his gaze, my stomach bottoms out and the heat simmering low in my belly flames as though he poured gasoline down my throat instead of his semen.

He rubs his thumb over my bottom lip and studies my face with hooded eyes.

"Let me taste myself on your tongue."

The deep, guttural quality of his voice obscures his words, but when I register what he means, heat rushes to my face. Yet as he lowers his head to mine, I don't pull away.

I should smack him, turn away, and remind him of his promises, but I can't. Not when he asks for permission and looks at me with such hungry eyes.

Especially not when I want another kiss from him.

His unhurried yet predatory approach steals the breath from my lungs, and when he groans in delight, wonder fills my chest.

I brought this terrifyingly huge and menacing man to the heights of pleasure.

The soft exploration of his tongue carries me away from reality as he deepens the kiss, and when he pulls away, urgency pulses through my clit.

"You're perfect, Aurora. I can't wait to taste every inch of you, so let's finish this thing with our parents and go sign some papers," he murmurs against my lips.

I shiver and nod.

He chuckles and pushes me toward the sink with a hand on my ass.

I turn on the faucet and absently cup some water into my mouth as he tucks his cock into his underwear and rights his trousers. My mouth waters at the intimate act, but I mentally kick myself and focus on erasing evidence of the last few minutes as best I can.

After running my hands through my hair, I count it a loss and tie it up with the hair band on my wrist.

Since my purse is at the table, I don't have my makeup, but after washing my hands and splashing water onto my face, I dab dry with the hand towel and pull my lipstick out of my pocket.

I pause and stare at my reflection in shock. My lips have never been so swollen, my cheeks have never been so flushed, nor have my eyes sparkled so brightly. After my sleepless night, fretful morning, and stressful afternoon, I expected to look pale and withdrawn, but I look more alive than ever before.

I swallow and apply a light coat of lipstick before tucking it back into my pocket and turning to meet Giorgio's gaze. The appreciation in his eyes confounds me.

Without a word, he tucks me against his side and leads me into the dining room, but when I try to return to my original spot, he tugs me closer and guides me to the chair beside his. I stiffen and try to pull away, but he ignores my attempts and pushes me down into the seat with firm yet careful hands.

My mother's glare sends ice down my spine.

After requesting the server change my place setting, Giorgio settles into his chair, picks up his drink, and leans back as though nothing happened.

I swallow and study his parents' faces. The crease between Bianca's eyes displays her unhappiness while Matteo's raised brows show his surprise. My father's tight smile sends dread through my limbs.

"Aurora, honey, are you alright?"

My mother's fake concern curdles my stomach. She's never once called me *honey* without a crowd. Bile rises in my throat.

Giorgio sets down his drink, and on impulse—and needing something to do with my hands—I pick it up and drain half the glass before my brain catches up with my movements.

Embarrassment heats my face at my audacity, but at least now the taste of vomit no longer lingers at the back of my throat.

As I set down the glass, Giorgio drapes his arm across the back of my chair and melts every molecule in my body with a scorching look. I swear my brain leaks right out of my ears, because I just stare at him like an idiot.

A harried server, full of apologies, breaks my stupor. I blink and peel my gaze away from Giorgio's and stiffen as I meet my mother's narrowed eyes.

"I'm fine, Mamma," I lie.

When awkward silence descends, I realize my parents don't dare question Giorgio despite their curiosity. Even his own parents hesitate.

He uses the opportunity to take over the conversation.

"Aurora and I spoke. She'll continue to live at home until after our wedding, but we'll sign a prenup this afternoon and start our efforts to grow our family as soon as possible."

No one moves for a moment. I fight the urge to shrink into my seat, unwilling to show an ounce of uncertainty when every individual in this room would happily bleed me dry and toss me aside without an ounce of guilt.

Everyone except Giorgio. I hope.

He's kept his word so far, and I want to trust him, so I put my faith in him. Kind of.

"*Mio fratello*, that's wonderful news. We also had a discussion while you were gone, and I think we raised some important issues," Bianca Vivaldi says.

My mother picks up the conversation.

"Aurora will visit your physician for a full workup in the morning, and since you're so busy, I'll go with her."

Her thinly veiled threat hits deep behind my sternum, but there's nothing more I can do to ensure my bloodwork comes back as normal. I haven't skipped a single dose of my medicine in years and feel as close to normal as I can. Plus, it's been almost seven years since I've had symptoms.

But there's always a possibility my numbers will be off enough to cause suspicion.

"I'll clear my schedule and take her myself. You don't need to join us."

I swing my attention to Giorgio, surprised by his response.

His stony expression brooks no argument, but my mother foolishly pushes. Realizing she may arouse more suspicion, I choose the path of least resistance and place my hand on Giorgio's thigh, ensuring I have his full attention.

"I'd like her to come, too. It'll be nice to have you both there."

It feels like the biggest lie I've ever told in my entire life, but I'll do whatever it takes to protect my brother from my mother's ire, and when I realize just how much of Giorgio's attention I have, the sour taste leaves my mouth. His dark eyes bore into mine as he leans a little closer and shifts his leg in my grip. The hard ridge of his cock nudges my fingertips.

"Since it's already so late in the day, why don't I book you an appointment with our lawyer for tomorrow morning after Aurora's physical? I think that's a better use of everyone's time instead of scrambling to meet the lawyer today," Matteo Vivaldi says.

Giorgio pulls his eyes away from mine and contemplates his father's offer before nodding. I wonder if anyone else notices his reluctance, but if they do, they don't show it.

With business matters settled, our parents move on to other topics. I thank the server for the new dishes and try to slip my hand off Giorgio's leg, but he reaches across his lap and pins my wrist in place. Among talk of wedding venues, flowers, and cake decorations, he drops his arm from the back of my chair, swaps hands, and feeds me food from his plate. Moths flutter in my abdomen, but I refuse to admit how much I enjoy his attentiveness, so I pretend to listen to the conversation.

Matteo stands, signaling the end of lunch, and pulls Bianca's chair out for her. Giorgio tightens his grip on my wrist and dabs his napkin over my lips. My insides clench as he allows the fabric to slip away. His thumb skims over my bottom lip. Lava pools between my legs as his eyes morph to melted dark chocolate. He pulls my lip down before trailing his fingers down the front of my throat.

When his knuckles brush against my breasts, I suck in a breath, but he plucks the napkin from my lap and tosses it onto the table before surging to his feet.

My legs wobble, but he pulls me to his side and hooks my hand over his forearm.

The stroll down the hall only reinforces how much bigger and stronger he is than me. I swallow and fix my purse over my shoulder as my parents hover by the front door, obviously waiting for me to say goodbye to our hosts, but

Giorgio gestures for them to lead the way down the hall without releasing my arm.

He escorts me down the stairs and opens the car door for me. Before I can slip into my seat, he pulls me flush against him and leans down to murmur in my ear.

"Sleep well tonight, *mia topolina*, because tomorrow I'm going to explore every inch of you over and over again, until there's no doubt who you belong to."

My mind blanks even as adrenaline and lust rush through my veins. I blink and blindly accept his help as he guides me into my seat. As reality teases the edges of my mind, I cling to the addictive sensations he spurred within me, avoiding the panic rising in me with every ounce of energy I have.

If I think about what just happened in that bathroom, I'll never be able to look at myself in the mirror again.

With my eyes open but seeing nothing, I ride in silence until my mother's voice breaks my stupor.

"I'll talk with you after our dinner reservation. Do not leave the house between now and then, unless someone from the Vivaldi family requests your appearance."

She doesn't wait for my response before accepting the attendant's hand and exiting the vehicle. I take a deep, steadying breath, and follow her into the horrorville I've called home my entire life.

With my mind reeling but the house too busy with the staff running through their chores to chance doing less legal tasks on my computer, I close myself in my room and take a quick shower. As I watch the bubbles disappear down the drain, part of me laments losing the lingering scent of Giorgio's cologne, but I shove the thought to the far corner of my mind and focus on surviving the evening.

Any thoughts of tomorrow will have to wait until tomorrow. I'm stretched too thin emotionally to handle more.

After dressing, I putter around my room for an hour or two, assuring myself the stashes of cash and other gear—most of which I realize won't be for me anymore—remain hidden as I pretend to clean. When I realize Tristan won't be home for another two hours, I settle in front of my computer and complete another week and a half of college assignments with relative ease, only opening my textbook a handful of times.

I slam my book closed and grind my teeth as a wave of futility washes over me.

My parents washed years' worth of studying down the drain in less than a day. My escape plan won't work, not without major changes. In fact, the secondary and emergency exits will only land my brother in a worse situation than he is now.

I power off my computer, avoiding any rash decisions, and push my chair in before sliding my phone in my back pocket and rushing out the side door to meet Tristan as he launches himself out of the van the second the attendant opens the door.

I thank Mr. Hearthright and, after a quick discussion, he agrees to extend tomorrow's activities until after dinner.

The band around my chest loosens as I enjoy Tristan's enthusiastic retelling of his day. He scarfs down dinner and bounces in his seat, eager to tell his online friends about his adventure. I soak up his happiness as I pick at my food, and after hanging out in his room for a little while, I realize I can't put off sharing this news for fear of our mother telling him in the most hurtful way possible.

"Hey, Tristan, I bet my day was crazier than yours."

He sighs, rolls his eyes, and bounces his ball off the wall again before responding.

"How can you say that when I already told you I fed a giraffe at the zoo today? Its tongue was *blue*, Rora. *Blue*."

"Oh, it's crazier than that," I say as I pretend to flip through the nearest book on his headboard.

"Really?"

I take a deep breath and prepare to rip off the theoretical Band-Aid now that I've piqued his interest.

"Yep. I'm getting married."

He purses his mouth in the most adorable display of disgust.

"Why would you do that?"

I shrug. He rolls his eyes.

"Mamma and Papà said you have to, didn't they?"

I nod.

"Well, did you meet him? Do you like him? Is he handsome? I'm going to marry someone pretty and smart, like you. Is he nice? Also, this is *not* as crazy as feeding a giraffe."

I laugh and toss the book onto his bedside table, relieved at his response.

"Yes, I met him. I'm not sure if I like him, but I guess he *is* handsome. And how is this not crazier? The giraffes are always at the zoo. I'll only get married once," I say, purposefully skipping whether or not Giorgio is nice and hoping Tristan doesn't notice.

He pauses his rhythmic tossing of the ball and tilts his head in thought.

"Just because something only happens once doesn't make it crazier, only rarer."

My heart gives a bittersweet squeeze. He's growing too fast. I cross my arms and give him a skeptical once-over.

"Who are you and what did you do with my brother?"

He sighs and rolls his eyes.

"Seriously, when did you get so smart?" I ask.

When our conversation devolves into fake insults and nonsensical teasing, I decide to drop the topic. He's obviously not ready to talk about how my wedding changes his future. I'll give him a day or two to digest the news before diving deeper into the specifics.

Hell, I'm not even sure right now. Fear closes my throat.

After a quick pillow fight, I wrap him in a hug and drop my cheek to the top of his head. I fight back tears as he hugs me back without hesitation.

He grumbles at my nagging, but I close his door and make it to the top of the stairs before a wave of emotion crashes over me. I lean against the wall, close my eyes, and regulate my breathing.

The front door opens. I meet my mother's eyes. Her face hardens. A bodyguard steps through the front door with my father staggering under his arm. Thankfully, the alcohol running through my father's veins slurs his words. With a disgusted scowl, my mother gestures for the man to take my father to his bed.

I press my back against the wall and offer both men a tight smile as they pass. My father doesn't even notice my presence. He's too lost in his own demons.

My heart pounds as my mother stops in front of me. When she motions for me to follow her without a word, dread forms like a rock in my stomach.

She stops in front of my room. I quietly release my breath, but she sticks out her upturned palm, so I slip my phone out of my pocket and hand it to her.

Instead of opening my door, she demands I follow her.

Tingling numbness rises from my toes when she stops in front of the utility closet.

She hasn't threatened to close me inside in five years, but her bitter expression tells me she won't change her mind this time. Cotton stuffs my ears and pressure builds in my head when she swings open the door and flicks on the light.

"You refused to fuck Giorgio Vivaldi, didn't you?"

The cotton muffles her words. I stare at the two unused yoga mats—one pink for my mother and the other blue for my father—rolled in the back corner of the closet.

"No man who sticks his dick in a woman stays as interested as he was during lunch. You're stringing him along, aren't you?"

I can't refute nor agree with her. My vision narrows and memories sneak closer.

"You're acting out because you're afraid of getting pregnant, aren't you? Even after I told you to behave."

The air thins.

"Get in."

I can't move.

"Get in before I drag your brother out to join you."

I shuffle forward on legs made of rubber. She shuts and locks the door behind me.

I'm okay. She didn't toss me in. I walked in on my own two feet. There's no screaming outside. Bright fluorescent light illuminates the space. Linens and cleaning equipment line the shelves instead of canned goods. My brother's tiny infant body isn't weighing down my arms. He's in his room. Comfortable. Safe. I'm okay.

I'm not okay.

The walls close in. Pressure builds in my head.

I tuck my back into the corner beside the yoga mats and curl into a ball. My mind splinters. I press both hands over my mouth and sob, but no tears flow down my face.

If I make noise, they'll find us. They'll kill us. We'll scream and beg for them to stop, but they won't. They'll laugh and hurt us even worse. They'll hit and threaten us until we can't scream anymore.

Just like they did my aunt.

CHAPTER 8

Giorgio Vivaldi

I SWING INTO THE PHYSICIAN'S parking lot thirty minutes early and sigh when Fiero's info pops up on the dash. With an aggravated jab at the touchscreen, I answer his call and snap out a *what* in greeting.

"You're fucking joking, right? That's what your dad called you home for yesterday? You're getting married?"

I grunt an affirmation as I pull into a spot and throw the car in park.

"Who's the unlucky broad?"

"Excuse me?"

"I mean, no shade to the future missus, but she'll be stuck with your sorry ass for the rest of her life, so she must've used up all her good luck already."

"You're only comfortable saying that because we're on the phone," I snarl.

"Damn straight, *stronzo*, especially with the last six months still fresh in my mind," he says with an exaggerated mock shiver into the phone.

I sigh and flip down my visor.

"So, who is it?" he asks.

"Aurora Achilles."

As the silence stretches between us, I check my hair in the mirror.

"The girl who yelled at you and then fainted in your arms at the Moretti/Taddeo wedding? Didn't her parents ship her overseas to never be seen or heard from again? When did she come back to New York?"

"Apparently she never left," I snarl.

"What? How?"

"They homeschooled her."

"Only her? As far as I know, Tristan Achilles is going to a private school."

"And how do you know that?"

He sighs, and in my mind's eye, I see him running his hand through his hair in exasperation.

"It's the Achilles family. One of New York City's founding mafia families. Tristan is Horatio's heir. Keeping track of them is hella easy when you're just a Vivaldi soldier nobody notices."

I grit my teeth, frustrated at my lack of information.

"Don't beat yourself up over not knowing. I mean, there's a reason everyone waits to gossip until you're out of earshot."

"So, you're saying I'm purposefully kept in the dark because I'm Matteo Vivaldi's heir?"

"Yep. It's part of who you are."

"Fuck that. Tell me everything you know. Dig into her situation. Past and present. I need all the information you can give me."

"You got it, boss. Want me to start now, or…"

As he sarcastically trails off, a black SUV turns into the parking lot.

"No, later. See if you can figure out why her parents might be desperate for a grandchild, too."

"Wait, they want you to—"

I end the call and open my door as Madona Achilles emerges from the back passenger seat. Nearest to the office door, she waits on the sidewalk as the driver rushes around to open the other side. I close my door and engage the alarm before heading toward them.

My steps falter as Aurora exits the vehicle. Despite her flawless makeup and the dress hugging her curves, her vacant eyes and wooden movements can't belong to the intelligent, sassy woman I met yesterday.

Was it only yesterday I felt her soft lips wrapped around my cock for the first time? It seems forever ago, yet each detail remains vivid in my mind.

I curse my overeager cock and ignore the restriction of my trousers as I close the distance between myself and my future bride.

She doesn't notice when I take her hand from the driver. Doesn't pull away when I guide her around the rear of the vehicle. Doesn't react when I stop in front of her mother.

"Aurora, did you say good morning to Giorgio?" Madona asks.

Aurora startles and checks her surroundings with wide eyes. A blush colors her too-pale cheeks as she realizes I hold her hand.

"*Mio Dio*, I'm sorry. I didn't sleep well and now I'm struggling with basic functions." She glances at her mother before squaring her shoulders and meeting my eyes. "Good morning. I'm glad you could join us, even though you must be busy."

I don't like it. Something is wrong. Very wrong.

I cup her chin and watch as several emotions flash across her features.

"Of course, I'm here. I'd do anything for you, Aurora," I say, mainly because it's true, but partially to gauge the reactions of the Achilles women.

Aurora doesn't believe me yet, but she will soon, while a hint of disgust slips through

Madona's polite mask. I note the change and focus on Aurora.

"Still, thank you. It means a lot."

I can't tell if she's telling the truth or putting on a show for her mother, so I kiss her on the forehead and tuck her against my side.

Her lack of spunk as I lead her into the office and follow the doctor to the little nook used to draw blood worries me. When I guide her to sit in the chair with a hand on her shoulder, she settles without fuss and lowers the arm rest as though she's done so a million times. After draping her arm over the padded bar, exposing the crook of her elbow, she looks around with unhappy eyes before reaching up with her other hand and weaving her fingers into mine.

Surprise sharpens my senses. Her show of trust nearly brings me to my knees, even as my mind screams for her to run away from me as fast as possible. I'm the last person she should trust after the way I failed my sisters, but I can't deny her the support when she so willingly reached out to me, so I give her digits a reassuring squeeze and sidle closer, offering her my bulk to lean her head on if she wants.

The nurse chatters away as she draws blood. At first, I worry her bubbly personality will annoy the shit out of me, but when Aurora slowly animates, I thank the woman for her thoughtful play-by-play as she explains what she's doing and the distraction she provides as she makes small talk. After filling several small vials with Aurora's blood, the nurse thanks us for our patience before disappearing down the hall.

When the same male doctor as before leads us to a room and instructs Aurora to strip for an examination before trying to usher me out into the hall, I stop him with a raised hand.

"I'll remain in the room. You'll find a female doctor and will not return today. I can't promise your safety if I see your face again this visit. *Capisci?*"

His audible swallow satisfies the beast lurking within me. He rushes to agree with me and hurries from the room.

I don't know how my father settled for such a pushover physician. If I had my way, I'd never see the weasel again. Ever.

Is this the same man who helped bury the trauma my older sister Camilla had to endure?

I turn to Madona, paste a smile on my face, and hope my cold lethality doesn't shine from my eyes.

If this woman hurt Aurora, she'll never lay eyes on her again. I don't care if she's her mother. No one will touch my woman but me.

"Thank you for bringing her this morning. I drove here, so she can ride with me for the rest of the day. I'll drop her off at home before dinner," I say.

She takes the hint and gracefully excuses herself as she backs out of the room. I half turn, feigning disinterest, and catch the warning look she sends Aurora before she starts down the hall. My hackles rise. I shut the door and twist the lock.

When I turn toward Aurora and find her expression closed off again, I grit my teeth and take an intimidating step toward her.

She fiddles with the gown folded on the table, but holds my stare.

I'll never figure out what's bothering her while she hides behind her emotionless mask, so I use the tactics that worked yesterday.

"Do you hate the thought of marrying me that much?" I say with another measured step closer.

She blinks and slowly digests my words.

"No, I don't. I just—"

"Are you dreading sleeping with me that much?" I interrupt.

Her eyes flit around the room as she realizes her predicament. She takes a tiny step backward and shakes her head.

"No, I—"

"Then what did your mother do to you?" I say, now almost in reaching distance.

"Nothing! I told you, I just didn't sleep well, so—"

"Prove it," I demand.

She halts mid-step and searches my face, no doubt recalling what happened the last time I spoke those words.

"H-how?"

"Strip. Take off all your clothes. Leave nothing covered. I need to see every inch of you."

She flicks a glance toward the door, but the determination in her glare assures me she won't bolt. Even if she does, no one will bat an eye if I chase her down and toss her over my shoulder.

She's mine.

"Fine, but—" I watch in fascination as she brushes against me on her way across the room. She picks up a chair from beside the door and drops it near the head of the exam table before stomping to the other side and pointing at the empty seat. "You sit there the entire time, and you'll keep your hands to yourself." She crosses her arms over her chest in the most impertinent and standoffish pose a woman has ever dared to take with me. "And I'm not touching you, either."

Satisfied she's somewhat back to her feisty self, I smirk and trail my fingertips over the table as I approach her.

Her pupils shrink. She steps back only to press against the wall.

"It still seems like you're dreading having sex with me," I taunt.

She shakes her head. I reach for the buttons on the front of her dress. She swats my hand away.

"I'm not, but you promised to protect me. Are you breaking your word?"

I can't stop my smirk from widening into a smile. Her fire fills me with delight.

"Alright, *mia topolina*. I'll sit. I'll watch. I'll keep my hands to myself. Just. This. Once."

She watches me with a skeptical expression as I ease my way backward to the chair, maintaining eye contact and waiting to finish my speech until after I plant my ass.

"But next time, I'll make you pay for teasing me."

Her sharp inhale expands her lungs and presses her breasts against the fabric of her dress. My mouth waters and heart pounds as she glares at me and clenches her fists at her sides.

"It's not my fault you refuse to leave the room, so no, you will not *make me pay* for *anything*. *Capisci?*"

An addiction forms. Lust hardens my cock faster than ever before as she stands her ground, all but daring me to squash her.

I need this. I need her.

This is a level of trust I never thought I'd earn from anyone, much less the angry little mafia princess who fainted at my feet six years ago.

She risked only her pride when she reached out to hold my hand before her blood draw, but by challenging me now, she risks her physical well-being along with her entire future.

Knowing I don't deserve her but needing to earn her trust, I settle back in the chair and cross my arms over my chest.

She sighs and kicks off her sandals.

When she unbuttons the top button of her dress, I growl and tilt my head, indicating she move to my side of the exam table. After a moment of petulance, she strides to stand several paces beyond the foot of the table, far out of reach but in full view of my hungry eyes.

I can't help but brace my knees further apart, requiring more room for my hard, throbbing cock, but despite the need roaring through me, I remind myself why I'm torturing myself like this.

Remembering her mother's scowl cools my ardor.

Even as she strips with impersonal, efficient movements, I struggle to breathe as she reveals more of her curves. She shrugs her dress off her shoulders and uses the table for balance as she steps out of the fabric before folding and placing it on the counter.

My mouth waters. I want to peel her black, lacy bra and panties off with my teeth, but the material accentuates her curves so well it seems a shame to take them off before I have the chance to fully appreciate them.

I keep one arm tucked against my front, but bring my other fist to my mouth and bite my knuckle, needing the sting to remain in my seat.

She reaches behind her back and unclasps her bra with practiced ease, but her lips flatten in a grimace as she brings her arms in front of her.

"Where are you hurt, Aurora?"

Even as I ask, she smacks her folded bra on the counter and tucks her thumbs into the waistband of her panties.

Her high, pert breasts barely wobble as she pushes her panties down her legs and steps out of the tiny scrap of fabric.

Words elude me as she folds her undergarment as though I'm not even in the room and sets it on top of her other clothes. Completely nude except for the tape and cotton ball in the crook of her arm, she squares her body with mine and stands with her feet shoulder-width apart and her arms out beside her.

I cannot breathe. She's perfect.

"No bruises. No scars. No abuse," she says as she rotates her arms to show me the other sides.

Unable to help myself, I pull my knuckle away from my teeth and draw a tiny circle in front of me, demanding she spin around.

She sighs and rolls her eyes—actually *rolls her eyes*—before following my silent demand.

When I find nothing but smooth, tempting skin, I nod toward the gown and focus on regulating my breathing as my eyes follow her every move.

Mio Dio, my cock has never been so hard before. I've never wanted someone so viscerally before, either. I don't know why our parents are conniving to see us married, but I'm extremely grateful they are.

She puts on the oversized gown and overlaps the flaps at the front before unlocking the door and pulling out the second step attached to the table.

Her glare warns me against offering help, and honestly, I might lose control if I so much as move a single muscle, so I remain as still as a statue even as the new doctor waltzes into the room.

The female proves kind, efficient—maybe a little too efficient for my taste—and unbiased throughout the entire examination. When she props her hip on the counter and finishes typing her findings on her laptop, I expect her to say the visit is over, but she clicks to a different screen and announces she has the results for Aurora's basic bloodwork.

My future bride stops fiddling with the paper blanket draped over her lap and gives the physician her full attention. Something in her expression catches my eye, but she smooths her features in a calm mask before I can decipher what it means.

"Everything looks fine except your iron levels. A point or two lower and we'd consider you anemic, but it's nothing to worry about," the doctor says, assuring Aurora when she stiffens. "We can get you within normal range with an iron supplement and by increasing your intake of leafy green vegetables, red meat, and things like iron-enriched cereals."

Aurora nods and thanks the doctor, who then says she's free to dress and we can leave whenever we're ready. After she closes the door behind her, Aurora turns a quizzical gaze my way.

"I'm not moving until you're back in that dress," I snarl.

With a scowl and a shrug, she hops off the table and puts her back to me as she pulls her panties on without taking off the gown. I watch in frustrated amazement as she snaps her bra into place and works her dress up her legs without offering me more than a glimpse of her pale flesh as she slips back into her clothes. She flings the gown onto the table, steps into her shoes, and snags her purse from the chair beside the door before meeting my gaze.

I surge from the chair and stalk toward my prey.

CHAPTER 9

Aurora Achilles

EVEN THOUGH I KNOW it won't deter him, I fling open the door and step backward into the hall. His lithe prowling melts my insides, counter-acting the jittery mess left behind by my nightlong panic attack, and his intense, dark eyes bore into my soul. He's too handsome in his laid-back business attire with the sleeves of his button down rolled up to reveal his tatted forearms. My heart pounds against my sternum and my head spins as I struggle to keep my balance, but when he hooks his arm around my waist and tugs me against him, the buzzing in my ears stops.

His warmth seeps into my flesh and begins my thaw. It feels like a lifetime since I last felt warm. I should push him away, but I neither have the energy nor the strength to deny myself the pleasure of his kiss as he lowers his lips to mine. His hard, demanding mouth dominates my senses until nothing exists beyond his teeth and tongue.

When he stops and pulls away, my mind remains blissfully silent.

A crease forms between his brows. He cups my face and brushes his thumb over my cheek, smearing the tears I didn't even realize had formed. I manage a shaky breath and close my eyes.

"Aurora, what—"

"If I can't say your name, then you can't say mine, either."

I don't know where the words come from. A thrill always runs down my spine when he says my name. Yesterday, I thought it was because he annoyed and scared the shit out of me, but today, with my defenses decimated, it feels like so much more. I like it but don't know why.

"You're trembling," he murmurs.

"I'm fine."

"No, you're not, but you're obviously not going to tell me why, even if I ask."

I can't refute him since it's true. I don't know him well enough to reveal such a massive weakness. If my own mother will use my fears against me, what would he do with such knowledge?

"I told you; I didn't sleep well."

"I believe you. I'm also aware there's more you're not telling me."

A nurse clears her throat from a few feet away. Blood rushes to my face as embarrassment rises from my toes as I realize we're blocking the hall.

Giorgio apologizes and tucks me under his arm before leading me to the parking lot. Surprise rolls through me. I expected him to have a flashy sports car, but the sleek black sedan doesn't detract from his lethal mafia persona, either. He opens the passenger door and offers me his hand.

I take it.

After helping me lower into my seat, he bends and slips his forearm under my knees. I squeak in alarm, but he pivots me toward the front of the car and settles my feet on the floorboard. His hand lingers on my calf before he wraps his thick digits around my ankle.

"*Mio Dio*, how the hell are you so small and *fragile*?"

I shift my bag on my lap, partially insulted but mostly really, really turned on. His hand feels gigantic around my ankle and his quietly rumbled words hold awe and yearning.

He pulls away with obvious reluctance and shuts the door before skirting around the front of the car and wedging himself into the driver's seat.

Now I understand why he doesn't drive around in a sports car. He wouldn't fit.

After starting the car, he reaches for the shifter, but I grab his arm and blink at my wayward hand for a moment before my brain catches up.

"Wait, I… just a minute," I mumble before dragging my hand away from his warmth and opening my bag.

He lifts a brow when I pull out the papers my mother shoved at me at the last second with a hissed warning. I pass him the stack and tuck my hair behind my ear.

"My mother told me to use this for our prenup. I haven't read it yet, so I don't know what it says, but..." Sitting in the surprisingly comfortable seat with the car buffering us away from the world, the adrenaline keeping me alert wanes, so I just shrug and finish lamely. "We should write our own."

Gravity triples. I fight with my lashes until movement snaps me awake. He leans over me and opens the glove box.

"My father did the same."

He drops a manilla envelope into my lap. I stare at it for a moment before understanding seeps into me. My brain accepts the new information and works it into whatever code must be running in the back of my mind, because I speak words that actually make sense despite the fatigue tugging at my limbs.

"We should study these for clues why they're so desperate to marry us in a rush."

After an extended moment of quiet—or maybe I fell asleep without meaning to—Giorgio agrees with me and puts both stacks into the glove box.

"We're not going to my father's lawyer," he says.

I jolt awake and meet his gaze. My belly flips at the unreadable expression on his face.

"Why?" I ask.

"I have my own, but her office is a few more streets north, so just relax for a bit. I'll wake you when we get there."

"Are you sure?"

"Of course, *mia topolina*."

"Why?"

"I need you awake and ready for the wicked things I plan to do to you."

Magma boils in my core, scorching my frozen, jumbled insides, and in my mania, I smirk and lean my head back.

"It seems I'm safe for now, then, because I am beat."

Despite—or maybe because of—Giorgio's presence filling the vehicle, I drop into an exhausted sleep without warning. When phantom screams ring in my ears, I reach out, terrified I lost my brother in the darkness, and sigh in relief when thick, masculine fingers weave within mine. Even though I know they aren't Tristan's, I cling to the hand as though the owner may lead me to safety.

I trust Giorgio Vivaldi on a soul-deep level. Maybe I shouldn't, but I do. I don't know if it's because first impressions have lasting effects, or if more recent events have led me to believe he's someone I can lean on.

Which might be why, when my senses slowly return to the corporeal world, I find my head resting on his shoulder. In my sleep, I leaned over the center console and wrapped myself around his arm. With his fingers still woven in mine, our hands in my lap, and all the weight of my upper body on his shoulder, he can't be comfortable, but he maneuvers through the busy city streets as though he doesn't have a woman plastered to half his body.

I sit up and wipe my face, horrified when drool smears over my chin.

He refuses to release my hand, and I can't force my fingers to let him go, so I fumble around in my bag with my nondominant hand until I find my tissues. I wipe my face and tug a few fresh ones out of the box before dabbing at the wet spot I left on his shoulder.

"I'm so sorry," I say in a voice still thick with sleep.

"I'm not."

His unexpected response steals the rest of my apology. I swallow and wish I had a bottle of water to clear my throat. After drying his shirt as best I can, I shove the used tissues into a side pocket of my bag and look out the window for the first time.

As I recognize several buildings and where we are in relation to his father's physician's office, skepticism clears away the last dregs of sleep from my mind. Shadows span over the streets, but not in the right direction for morning. A glance at the dash shows we're way past lunchtime.

Alarm surges through me. I meet Giorgio's eyes.

"I thought you were going to wake me when we got to your lawyer's office?"

He lifts a brow and smirks before returning his attention to the windshield.

"We're not there yet, so there was no need to wake you."

I blink.

Did he drive around in circles for hours just so I could sleep?

I discard the thought. There's no way Giorgio Vivaldi would do something so nice. Not for me. Not when he's made it perfectly clear he's eager to sign prenups just so he can have his way with my body.

I clear my throat and shift in my seat.

Which is a mistake. His fingertips brush along the inside of my bare thigh. My heart leaps into my throat and lust pools low in my belly, but when I try to lift our joined hands away from my lap, he growls and shifts his fingertips higher up my leg.

I freeze.

Silence presses down on my head. Whatever special soundproofing he must have had installed works a little too well. It blocks out the sounds of the city, even the yelling cab drivers and honking horns.

He pulls into a small parking garage and continues down to a lower level. I try not to grind my teeth when a quick calculation leads me to believe the physician's office was less than twenty minutes away.

I don't understand this man. At all.

My stomach rumbles. A blush creeps up my chest and heats my ears. He glances at me before pulling into a spot and putting the car in park.

I decide it's annoying how easily he controls the car with only one hand, even as my libido demands he's the most attractive and capable man I've ever seen.

He squeezes my hand and sneaks his pinky higher up my thigh. An embarrassing squeak escapes my throat and I use both hands—and all my upper body strength—to push him away from my sex.

My damp panties mock me.

When he angles his shoulders as much as he can in the cramped space and pins me in place with his intense stare, I expect him to pull me to him for a kiss, but he reaches across the center console and cups my face.

The world shifts as his expression softens, and without a word, he steals chunks of my idiotic heart.

I stare in mute shock as he pulls away, extracting his hand from mine, and exits the car. When he opens my door but doesn't offer me his hand, I look up at him.

"Bring both sets of papers. We'll look through them together."

I nod and slip them into my bag before accepting his help to exit the car.

When he settles his arm over my shoulders and weaves his fingers through mine, a sense of belonging nearly knocks me off my feet, but with his massive frame pressed against mine, there's nowhere for me to fall. I fill my lungs and savor the scent of his cologne with hints of his natural musk woven within.

He leads me into an elevator. His eyes constantly scan our surroundings, reminding me we're alone in public together for the first time.

Even when the elevator doors close and offer a blurred reflection of us, he stays alert, checking corners for surveillance cameras and pulling me close.

He's so tall and muscular compared to my petite frame. It's a wonder the elevator can even handle his weight. He's pure muscle. It's intimidating.

He leads me out of the elevator before I'm ready. Discombobulated, I speak before my brain catches up.

"This isn't a lawyer's office."

God, I could smack my stupid mouth.

He grunts and asks for a quiet table for two. The hostess immediately gestures for us to follow and leads us through the restaurant to a table in the corner. He places me in the corner and takes the chair next to mine, boxing me in. After asking what drink I want, he orders a few appetizers before allowing the waitress to sashay away.

Jealousy swarms behind my sternum as she exaggerates the swing of her hips for Giorgio as she departs, but when I turn to him, he's staring at me. My heart lurches when he quirks a brow.

I tell myself I'm allowed to act a bit unhinged after the drama of the last day and a half. Hell, I sucked his cock during my first ever sexual altercation. It's understandable I'm attached.

He pushes my menu toward me. I duck my head and stare at the simple, elegant list but struggle to make sense of the words.

When he asks what I want, I force myself to focus and choose what sounds easiest to digest—since my stomach seems set on lurching every other second—and my entire nervous system seems stuck in an overactive state.

As the appetizers arrive, he drapes his arm over the back of my chair in response to the waitress' flirting and dismisses her before turning to me.

"Do you have any food allergies? Anything you hate?"

I shake my head and eye him skeptically as he reaches for a roll. When he holds a piece to my lips, I consider my options before accepting it.

The waitress glares at me as she leaves. Giorgio smirks.

Despite me insisting I can feed myself, he ferries food to my mouth, sometimes pinched between his fingers and other times on a utensil. Too befuddled and wary of making a scene, I don't balk even when he brushes crumbs off my lips with his thumb, and I fumble to comply when he suggests I place the papers on the table.

We skim through the legal jargon as we eat, but most of the terms seem rote, so nothing jumps off the pages at us.

When he orders dessert, I send him an exasperated glance before blocking his next attempt to feed me.

"I'm done. My stomach is going to explode, so stop trying to cram more food down my throat," I demand.

His chuckle sends shivers down my spine.

"I'm not cramming anything down your throat. Not yet, anyway."

My heart quickens, and I fight against the urge to wriggle in my seat as my clit pulses. I shake my head, push his hand away, and pick up my drink as an excuse to put distance between us.

After a few minutes of silence, he picks up the stack from my mother and leans so close I have no choice but to hold his stare.

"What do *you* want from our prenup, Aurora?"

I swallow and set down my glass as I gather my thoughts.

"I want your assets to remain yours and my assets to remain mine, no matter what happens."

"Even if I knock you up and leave you, you wouldn't want any of my money or power?"

The intensity in his eyes terrifies me, but I answer as honestly as possible without revealing too much.

"I'm not afraid of raising a child on my own, but raising a child on my own while losing everything I've built for myself? Terrifying."

I don't shy away as he studies me.

"What have you built for yourself, *mia topolina?*"

When my initial fury fades away, I realize he isn't mocking me. The curiosity in his bottomless brown orbs tempt me to reveal everything, but I stop myself before I ruin everything.

"I have a few bank accounts my parents don't know about."

It's the truth. Mostly.

"And how do you have that?"

I shrug and play with the condensation on my glass.

"Raised on a computer, remember?"

After an unnerving amount of time, he accepts my answer with a nod. The waitress brings dessert. I try to resist, but after avoiding sweets for most of my life, I'm powerless against the warm chocolate cake and creamy ice cream combo as he sneaks it into my mouth.

I haven't eaten so much in years. As I fight against slipping into a food coma, he pays the bill, leads me into the elevator, and introduces me to his lawyer before settling me onto the couch in her office. When he sits beside me, the cushion dips, but I scoot toward the armrest and sit ramrod straight.

I try to stay alert, I really do, but when the lawyer proves friendly yet clearly professional and uninterested in Giorgio as anything other than a client, my attention wanes. They go over what our parents included in their drafts, only to discard most of it and begin altering a basic template to meet our terms.

The comfortable couch, my full belly, last night's trip to nightmarelandia, and Giorgio's rich voice all work against me. I slip into a doze. When muscular arms wrap around me and pull me against a hard body, I snuggle closer, needing more of his delicious scent and enticing warmth.

I jerk awake and frantically wipe at my mouth, terrified of a repeat performance in the drool department. Thankfully, my chin proves dry, so I swallow my embarrassment and focus on the lawyer. She hands me a few pieces of paper.

All the air leaves my lungs as I read through them. My hands shake the more I read. Disbelief spears through me.

He can't mean this.

But his initials and signature are already dry on the document.

If anything happens—anything, be it his fault, my fault, a mutual decision, or a catastrophic event like his death—everything becomes mine. Everything. His stocks. His company. His role in the family business. His dependents.

With my heart in my throat and my mind running a million miles a second, I look to Giorgio, certain he'll tell me this is all a joke.

It must be a joke. No one who has as much to lose as he does would sign something like this.

No one.

CHAPTER 10

Giorgio Vivaldi

HER ADORABLE EYES stamp themselves into my psyche. Few things in life have ever swayed me from my original path, but I'd go in any direction she pointed. Without hesitation.

She works her bottom lip between her teeth before huffing and lifting the papers closer to my face.

"This joke isn't funny," she says.

I quirk a brow and squeeze her hip.

"It's not a joke," I respond.

"Oh yeah, sure. You—Giorgio Vivaldi, the heir to the Vivaldi fortune—are willingly signing your entire life's work over to me."

"I am," I say without hesitation.

"This makes no sense!"

The exasperation in her voice, which is still throaty from sleep, amuses me to no end.

"It doesn't need to."

"That's the dumbest response I've ever heard. Why would you do this?"

I shrug and enjoy watching her features as she struggles to process what this means.

"You're not planning on committing suicide, are you?"

Before I can answer, she stuns me with an even more ludicrous scenario.

"Or planning to fake your death and leave me with all your horrible mistakes, including a dozen bastards by different women, so you can disappear into the sunset and retire on a beach somewhere without a care in the world, are you?"

"Damn, why didn't I think of that?" I murmur, just to watch her scrunch her nose in frustration.

"This *is* a joke to you, isn't it?" She turns to my lawyer. "This signature isn't valid because he's mentally unstable, right? He *can't* give me everything, can he?"

"I can and I will," I say.

She gives the cutest growl and swings her vibrant green orbs up to mine.

"You're just being a jerk again, aren't you? Stop mocking me. I cannot handle—"

I weave my fingers into her hair and pull her against me. It's a little awkward on the couch, but she still fits perfectly in my arms.

"I'm not mocking you, *mia topolina*. If you're going to inherit the dangers and risks that come with marrying me, you're going to accept all the perks, too. *All* the perks. Every. Last. One."

Her pupils dilate and red stains her cheeks at my innuendo. I trail my thumb over her face, enjoying the warmth of her blush.

"I didn't ask for this," she whispers.

"I know," I say.

"I don't want this," she states.

"I know."

Her lack of interest and the trust she showed me when she fell asleep beside me—twice— sealed my decision.

"Then *why?*"

"There is no why. It just is."

She sighs, glances at the papers in her hand, and sends me a fresh scowl. I continue before she asks why again.

"I have no ulterior motive, Aurora. You asked for my protection. This is the only way I can assure you have it."

After searching my face, she sighs yet again and drops her forehead to my chest, pulling her hair from my loose grip. I give her a moment to process before wrapping my fingers around her nape.

She lifts her head and pierces my soul with her animated emerald eyes.

"Fine, but if you disappear or die, I'll devote every ounce of power and spend every cent on either finding or reviving you, just so I can kill you myself."

It's not the response I expected, but I was an idiot for expecting anything less. I let my amusement and adoration play on my face and smile.

"Of course, *mia topolina.*"

She elbows me as she faces the table. With more force than necessary, she slaps the papers onto the desk, snatches a pen from the center of the table, and scribbles where my lawyer instructs.

"We're not taking actual paper copies of this, are we?" Aurora asks.

She's too fucking smart.

"No, we're not. This is a private document. It'll never leave Mrs. Tamsin's safe."

"No electronic copies?"

"We keep scans of every document on a local database," the woman says.

"Do you mean a local hard drive?" When my lawyer looks as lost as I do, Aurora continues. "Databases don't store data, they analyze it. Do you have an actual device that stores the files here, or are they sent to a cloud or external storage provider?"

"I… I'll have to check," Mrs. Tamsin says.

"There's no point for either of those. If you have a fireproof safe, then just keep this copy in there. Don't scan it," Aurora demands.

When Mrs. Tamsin looks torn, I lean my elbows onto my thighs and take Aurora's hand.

"Give me a notarized copy. No scan, just a copy. I'll keep it in my safe."

Aurora's fingers stiffen in mine.

"You are *not* taking that into the Vivaldi family home. Or into any workspace or office where you conduct business."

"You're right. I'm not."

"Then where are you putting it?"

"My townhouse. The address is listed on the document."

"Just because it's yours doesn't mean it's safe. What if your father—"

"My father doesn't know it even exists. He may drive by it now and then, but it means nothing to him. He has no interest in that part of the city."

"Are you sure?"

"Why do you think I picked it?"

She chews on her bottom lip as she digests the information, then gives a nod of acceptance.

"I'm okay with that, I think. You promise you aren't trying to get me killed? If anyone knows this exists—"

"This is between the three of us. No one else will know unless *you* tell them," I assure her.

"Okay. I trust you."

My heart aches. She shouldn't trust me, not after I failed my sisters. I cup her face in my hands and brush my lips over hers, but pull back when she gasps. I won't be able to stop at just a taste, and my lawyer's office is not where I want to take her virginity.

In fact, after watching her sleep for hours and still look exhausted, guilt creeps through me for even considering acting out my lewd fantasies. I'll survive another day if I don't slake my lust, but there's no guarantee she'll continue to trust me if I push her too hard.

I can't lose her trust. I need it.

I tuck her against my side and lean back on the couch to wait for the lawyer to return with my copy of the paperwork. She remains stiff for a moment, but leans into me when I tighten my arm over her shoulders.

"You already gave me this much, *mia topolina*. Don't take it away now."

She aims quizzical eyes up at me, but the only lawyer I trust in New York City returns. I take the folder from her and rise, keeping Aurora plastered to my side, and thank the businesswoman before ushering my prize to the elevator. On high alert, I catalogue Aurora's every lithe movement while noting each potential danger until I settle her in my car and shut the door. As I stroll around the hood, I send Fiero a quick text, demanding he leave his keycard to my townhouse—the only spare I have—on the kitchen counter in the next ten minutes before I drop into the driver's seat and hit the ignition.

We make the drive in silence. Aurora barely moves as she watches the world outside the windows, and when I notice her keeping track of street names and familiar buildings, pride flows through my chest but tension coils through her when I open the electric gate and turn onto my townhouse's narrow lot. Her eyes widen in shock as I pull into the single-car garage—a rarity for townhomes—and I wonder how she'll look in the throes of passion. The gate and the garage door automatically close behind us.

"This is where you live?" she asks.

I nod, not trusting my voice. My phone chimes and Fiero's text message displays on the dash.

Of course, the bastard had to leave a no context, highly suggestive and damning message.

Aurora's eyes flash, but she turns away, hiding her face from me.

"Are you sure this place is safe?" she asks.

"Yes. The first thing I did when I bought it was upgrade the security."

My fingers itch to weave into her hair, but I grab my phone instead.

"Who is Fiero, and why did he have a key to your place?" she asks, still facing the window.

"He's the man I'd choose to make my second, if he'd agree to it."

She swings her eyes to my face.

"But isn't your uncle the Vivaldi consigliere?"

"He's my father's right-hand man, yes. Not mine."

Her eyes drift toward the windshield as she works through the gravity of my words. Despite the exhaustion and emotional anguish lurking in her eyes, she's still the most gorgeous woman I've ever seen.

"Fiero is loyal only to me, not my father, so you don't have to worry about anyone from my family finding out," I say.

"No one from your family knows?"

"Fiero and I are the only ones."

She nods, accepting my assurances.

I help her from the car and give her a quick tour of the house and back garden before leading her into the tiny office. She watches in pensive silence as I reveal the hidden safe and relay the passcode to her while I open it.

I step back and gesture for her to place the folder on whichever shelf she wants. She approaches as though she's afraid a snake will jump out and bite her, but after setting down the documents that detail how everything is hers, she turns and walks away without even checking the contents of the safe.

My phone chimes. I read the message and send a reply, welcoming the change of plans since the demon inside me kept picturing Aurora sprawled out on every surface as I gave her a tour of the house. Willing my cock to soften, I adjust myself before following my future bride into the kitchen.

I pluck the keys from the counter, place them on her palm, and curl her fingers around them.

"You're welcome here anytime, Aurora. Treat it as your own now. *Capisci?*"

Tears shimmer in her eyes. My heart hurts. I pull her to my chest and surround her with my bulk, silently promising to protect her from the world. I don't know what demons she's fighting, but I swear I'll decimate every one.

My cock pounds with need, but I cherish how she willingly accepts my comfort. When she gets her breathing under control—the stubborn woman refused to cry—she tentatively rests her hands on my sides.

Any more touching and I'll fuck her on the counter without the foreplay she deserves, so I grab her nape and push her toward the garage in front of me.

"Wait, where are we going?"

"Out."

"But I thought…"

"You thought I brought you here just to fuck you?"

"Why wouldn't I? You said the next time you got me alone, you'd—"

"Don't you think you've drooled on me enough today?" I interrupt, knowing I'll lose control if I hear her repeat the filthy words I said to her.

I open the car door and push her into the seat before reaching over her and latching her seatbelt.

The embarrassment staining her features is too tempting. I nip her bottom lip and lick her cheek before hovering my lips beside her ear.

"The answer is no, *mia topolina*. You could drool *all over* me, and I'd demand more. I want you so bad I've got blue balls from how hard I've been all day just from letting you nap on me."

I shut the door and settle behind the wheel, gritting my teeth when she squirms in her seat. After opening the garage and front gate, I put the car in reverse and look over my shoulder to navigate the tight drive.

"If you're like that, then why are we leaving?"

I block traffic for a moment, ensuring the gates close before shifting into drive, and settle my hand on her thigh. She jumps in surprise, but doesn't push me away.

"There's someone I want you to meet," I say.

She looks at me expectantly. I turn my attention to the road. She sighs and scoots back in her seat as though that'll stop my hand from inching up her leg.

I can't help it. I need to touch and tease her until she's desperate enough to beg.

She grows more apprehensive as I pass through each security checkpoint, and by the time I pull into the underground parking lot, she grips the door's armrest with white knuckles. I park in the space closest to the elevator and demand she wait for me with a warning squeeze to her thigh. She swallows and nods.

The urge to kiss her nearly wins, but I exit the vehicle and rush her to the elevators. When I wrap one arm around her waist and pull her to my side, she comes willingly. Her submission morphs even the most mundane act into an erotic tease.

I remain aware of our surroundings, unable to ignore the skills and instincts I've honed for years, but don't check for security cameras or potential threats. This building is one of the few places besides my townhouse and my parents' home where I don't have to worry about an attack.

"Is this a hotel?" Aurora asks as I mash the button for the penthouse.

"There are apartments in the building, but no, I'm not taking you to a hotel room."

The elevator chimes as we reach our floor. I step out and enjoy the brushing of our bodies as she walks beside me.

The door to the penthouse opens before we reach it.

Aurora falters as Nico Russo fills the doorframe.

"I didn't know you were bringing company," he scowls.

"I didn't tell you I was, but this is a face-to-face issue, so here we are," I say.

Even though I know he's happily married to my sister, I still tighten my arm around Aurora when he gives her a once-over.

"Why are you standing in the doorway? If Giorgio is here, then—"

Serenity elbows her way past Nico and stops mid-sentence as she notices Aurora. Her brows rise and she tilts her head for a moment.

"Aurora? You were just a kid the last time I saw you! How are you? And why are you here with my brother?"

Without waiting for a response, she takes Aurora's hand and pulls her away from me.

There are *very* few people I'd allow to come between me and my betrothed.

Serenity is one of them. She doesn't have a mean bone in her body and there's no way I can make up for how I've failed her.

Even with the dark edge of menace emanating from Nico's eyes, he watches my sister with the same emotions I feel budding in my chest for Aurora. With a sigh, he stops her from passing with a hand on her slightly rounded belly.

"You can recognize someone you haven't seen since childhood, but you can't remember the name of your bodyguard?"

Serenity sighs and pats his arm as she slips past.

"It's not on purpose, I swear. Remembering and learning are two completely different things, especially during pregnancy, so blame it on the hellion you planted in my belly, not me."

I chuckle and enjoy the flash of frustrated levity on Nico Russo's face until he meets my stare and recalls why he asked me here.

He might have a lead on who's behind the attacks on both our families.

CHAPTER 11

Aurora Achilles

I CAN'T SPEAK PAST the lump of emotions in my throat, but Serenity senses my upheaval and offers me a glass of water. I take it and use it as an excuse to delay my response. She fills the silence.

"I think the last time I saw you was at that godawful wedding several years ago, the one where half a dozen people passed out from heat exhaustion and went to the emergency room because some dumbass planned an outdoor wedding in the middle of summer. I'm sure the open bar didn't help, either."

"Wait, I wasn't the only one who fainted?"

"Oh no, you definitely weren't. But you *were* the only one Giorgio caught and carried all the way across that humongous venue to the ambulance. I've never seen my brother run so fast in my entire life."

"You're quite the chatterbox today, aren't you, Senny?" Giorgio says from behind me.

I miss Serenity's response as he joins me at the counter, standing so close his arm brushes over mine.

"Confinement looks good on you, though."

His teasing tone shocks me from the roots of my hair to the tips of my toes, followed closely by envy and yearning.

Serenity ignores him by pointing her focus at me.

"So why are you here, and what made you come with my brother?"

"We're getting married," Giorgio answers for me.

His lack of finesse in delivering the news both annoys and relieves me.

"Oh," Serenity hesitates and glances behind us before asking, "When?"

"In four months," Giorgio says.

"Well, that's terrifyingly familiar. Did Papà spring it on you the same way he did me?" she asks.

Disbelief spears through me. I saw Nico and Serenity's betrothal announcement and wedding invitations in my mother's emails and texts, but didn't look at the dates close enough to realize they married so quickly.

"It seems he's mastered the art of ambushing his children," Giorgio says.

Serenity's expression turns mutinous. She aims a glare behind us again. I glimpse Nico's reflection in the backsplash and realize he's leaning on the wall in the living room.

"We're changing Camilla's phone number and blocking our parents' information. They are *not* putting her through that. I don't care if she has to cut contact with them permanently. She—"

As Serenity continues her rant, I lower my eyes to the counter, feeling like an interloper witnessing something private and precious. I'm envious of her ability to voice her concern for her sister.

My long, lonely past stretches behind me. I wish I had a sister like her to protect me. Hell, any sibling near my age would be amazing, but the ten-year gap between Tristan and me makes our dynamic seem more like a mother and child.

I don't regret raising my brother—he's always been the best thing about my life—but the constant weight of responsibility, fear, and loneliness sometimes feels like too much to bear.

"Whatever you think is best," Nico says in response to Serenity's concern.

Her anger melts away and tears fill her eyes.

"Come here, *mia principessa*," Nico demands.

Serenity crosses the kitchen and disappears into his arms, mumbling about stupid hormones and babies and virile mafia men.

I jump when Giorgio's massive hand encompasses the back of mine on the glass.

"Squeeze any harder and you might break it," he murmurs.

My lame response is to squeak and slip my hand out from under his.

"I'm okay now. You called him over for a reason, so go take care of it," Serenity says with a final sniffle and a push out of her husband's arms.

When Nico reaches for her, she swats him away and starts toward us.

"That's your hint to get out of the room. It's time for girl talk," she tells Giorgio.

After an extensive study of my face, Giorgio tucks a stray hair behind my ear before following Nico into the study.

Serenity opens the fridge and systematically fills the counter with containers of food.

"I swear, as soon as our honeymoon ended, all I wanted to do was eat all day long. Snacks are easier to digest, maybe? There's plenty to share, so just grab a fork and dive in."

I stare at the options, too overwhelmed to move.

"I'm sorry, that's probably gross. Nico's had me in lockdown for a few weeks, so the probability of me being sick is basically in the negatives, but if you'd rather—"

I reach into the drawer and grab a fork before she can close it.

"No. Please. Thank you."

The right words won't form. Emotions threaten to bury me.

Serenity's slim yet strong arms wrap around me.

It's been almost a decade, but her hug hasn't changed at all.

I break. Ugly sobs. Tears. Snot. The whole shebang.

I don't know how she does it, but she completely unravels me. It could be her naturally sweet and caring nature, her unfettered welcome, her lack of pity, or the understanding—from her own personal experience, at that—in her gaze, but the pillars holding me up crumble.

She pats my back and hugs me tighter, just like she did when we were kids. The firmness of her belly only breaks me further.

I pull myself together by sheer force of will. Too many emotions batter me, so I shove them into tiny compartments to decode later and wipe my tears, but I can't force myself to leave Serenity's arms.

Realization hits me. I know why her embrace means so much to me.

She's the only person besides my aunt who ever hugged me.

Telling her so will only make me feel more pathetic—and reveal way too much about my predicament—but I need her to know how grateful I am. I can never repay her for these kind gestures.

After resting my forehead on her shoulder and soaking in as much of her as I can, storing her scent and the feel of her arms around me for later when I need encouragement, I fill my lungs and hold my breath until it hurts.

"Thank you, Serenity. A lot," I say as I pull away.

She scoots the tissue box closer. I snag a few.

"Better?" she asks.

I nod.

"Then dig in."

When she stabs her fork into the tub of spaghetti, I give her a wobbly smile and reach for what looks like spinach.

"Hey, if you're on a diet, no, you aren't." She pulls the spinach out of reach. "These calories don't count because they're for the baby. Eat whatever you want, not what you think you should eat."

I study the options.

"But that *is* what I want. Truly," I say when she gives me a skeptical look.

"You sure?"

I nod. She shrugs and passes it over.

"Careful, it's spicy. Like, melt your mouth spicy. Nico ordered it from an authentic Thai restaurant, I think."

"It smells amazing," I say before I take a bite. It tastes more than amazing, so I go for seconds. As I scarf down half the container, I choose my next victim. Serenity gives a happy wiggle and picks a bite from almost every box.

When I reach for my next choice, Serenity offers to warm it up on the stove, but I shovel it in my mouth and shake my head.

After the horrendous amount of food Giorgio pushed down my throat not long ago, I shouldn't be hungry, but a hole must have formed in the bottom of my stomach. I've never had much of an appetite, but I've also never had a chilled medium-rare steak before.

I pause mid-chew.

Fuck. Leafy green veggies. Red meat. Insatiable hunger.

My mother made sure I took my prescription this morning, but with the emotional upheaval, broken sleep, and mountains of stress heaped on top of my head recently, it's possible I'm not absorbing the nutrients I need.

Serenity clears her throat and nudges the steak toward me.

"No judgment here, Aurora."

"That's not it. I just… our parents want us to make a pregnancy announcement in less than a year."

She gasps and slams her fork onto the marble counter. I jump at the unexpected sound as it cracks through my ears.

A gigantic shape rushes past me. Nico snatches Serenity off her feet and pins her to the fridge.

Thick fingers weave into my hair and yank my head back as a massive arm wraps around my front and tugs me back against Giorgio's hard body.

"What happened? Where are you hurt?" he snarls.

"I-I'm not hurt," I say.

His melted dark chocolate eyes check me from head to toe before narrowing on my swollen eyes.

"You were crying," he accuses.

"She's allowed, Giorgio. *Mio Dio*, what is wrong with our parents?" Serenity hisses.

"You scared the shit out of me, *mia principessa*. Calm down and explain what your parents did this time," Nico demands.

"How old are you, Aurora?" Serenity asks.

"Eighteen," I answer.

"She's three years younger than Natalie! No. You can't. Giorgio, tell me you won't," she growls.

Before he's forced to anger his sister further, I respond.

"It's not his fault, Serenity. Neither of us has a choice, so don't take it out on him."

She takes a deep breath and shakes her head.

"No. You're not ready for a baby."

Her outrage on my behalf soothes all the pain caused by my parents. I still want their love and protection, but knowing there's someone in the universe who cares enough about me to fight for me erases the worst of my agony.

Even though she doesn't understand how dangerous pregnancy would be for me, she's still against me having a baby so young.

"Thank you. I mean it. Thank you."

My throat closes up, but I refuse to cry, so I swallow.

"Don't tell me there's a *but* after your gratitude," she snarls.

"There is. It's okay now. I trust Giorgio and I trust myself. We'll handle this how it needs to be handled."

"I think they will, too. You've been on your feet too long, *principessa*. Let's get you in bed," Nico insists.

"Don't go all high-handed on me right now. I'm pregnant, not sick, and we're in the middle of a conversation."

He scoops her into a cradle hold. She sighs.

"Naps are boring without my tablet. Why'd it have to go all *blue screen of death* right when I'm trapped at home?"

"What type of tablet is it?" I ask without thinking.

Serenity has already helped me so much; I can't leave her without entertainment if it's an issue I can fix.

Which I can. She answers my question, but it isn't important.

"Can I look at it? I'm pretty good at solving tech issues."

Giorgio's arm tightens around my stomach. Although he loosened his grip on my hair, he hasn't released me.

Shit. I'm not doing a very good job of hiding my interests if he's caught on after only a day and a half. I'll have to tread carefully, because if he knows what I'm truly capable of, he'll ruin any chance I have of getting Tristan to safety.

CHAPTER 12

Giorgio Vivaldi

AFTER NICO APPROVES Aurora's request to work on the tablet, he settles Serenity on the couch and stalks down the hall to retrieve it from their bedroom. I pull Aurora down onto the loveseat beside me.

"Do you remember what you were doing before the blue screen popped up?" Aurora asks.

"I was downloading updates on the design app my school requires for all students."

"Did any of the other students report issues?"

"I don't think so. The tech guy said maybe it's because I didn't update my tablet first, but I never saw a notification, and I always install the updates as soon as they roll out, so I don't know."

Aurora takes the tablet from Nico, but the creases on her forehead say she wouldn't notice even if a monkey handed it to her. She hits the power button and reads the warning.

When she shifts as though to stand, I slip my hand around her forearm and tug her back into the seat. She gives me an annoyed glance, but goes back to fiddling with the tablet as though nothing else exists.

I shouldn't call her cute, since some would say she's barely legal, but she's an intriguing mix of angelic and demonic as she ignores the rest of the world to pinpoint the issue.

When I finally pull my stare from her face, she's scrolling through a never-ending wall of white text on a black background. Surprise widens her eyes before she scowls and leans closer to the screen.

She understands more than she lets on. Tendrils of suspicion sneak through me, so I watch and catalog her every movement, but the

HTML code or whatever jargon she's reading may as well be in hieroglyphics to me.

I can torture a man without mercy, run a business without breaking a sweat, and navigate the ruthless mafia underworld without hesitation, but I can't do… whatever it is she's doing.

This is more than the average 'I was homeschooled' or 'I was raised on a computer' skill set. I meet Nico Russo's eyes. His attention sharpens as he picks up on my suspicion.

She flips and types, scans and swipes, and returns the tablet to the home screen within a few minutes.

Trained professionals take hours to work through what she just fixed. At Serenity's excited squeal as she hands it over, Aurora smiles.

My heart skips a beat. I want her to look at me with those caring eyes and that soft expression.

"I uninstalled the design app, but everything you had saved should still be in the school's cloud storage system. Your software is up to date, too, so maybe talk to a different technician to figure out what went wrong before you download the design app again."

As Serenity thanks her, Nico studies Aurora, as baffled as I am over her skills. I pull her to my side and wrap my arm around behind her to grab her hip.

Her elation fades when she glances at my face.

When Nico not-so-subtly tries to kick us out again, I say goodbye to my sister and pull Aurora toward the door. She pauses in the foyer and looks over her shoulder, but turns back around and exits the suite without another word.

I consider confronting her about my suspicions but decide to wait until she's comfortable telling me the truth, so I settle her into my car without a word and drive in silence. When she leans her shoulder against the door and sighs, I reach over the console and take her hand. Her fingers tremble as she gives me a squeeze.

Her sweetness may be the death of me.

After a few minutes, her lashes sweep down to rest against her cheeks.

Pride and awe swell within my heart. Every time she falls asleep in my presence, she steals a massive chunk of my soul.

I stop at the gate to our last destination for the day and roll down my window to talk to the guard. Aurora's hand twitches in mine when he speaks. The man welcomes me and waves me through the gate. I pull forward and park in the posh roundabout near the front entrance.

Unable to resist, I lift Aurora's hand to my face and brush my lips over the back.

"Wake up, *mia topolina*. I brought you home early, so you can go inside and rest."

She scowls and mumbles, still half asleep.

"Tristan won't be home until after dinner. I don't want to go in early." I pause before rubbing my lips back and forth over her knuckles.

"Why don't you want to go inside?" I murmur against her skin, keeping my voice low so she doesn't fully wake.

"We didn't have sex. She'll lock me in the closet again."

She gasps and jolts awake as I squeeze her hand in shock.

"Your mother locked you in the closet?"

My voice emerges as more of an animalistic rumble than actual words. After a moment of confusion, she glares at me in fury.

"You're such a jerk. Let me go. I—"

When she reaches for the door handle, my control snaps. I grab her by the hair and haul her over the center console and into my lap. She screams and flails, but I part her knees around my hips and trap her arms to her torso while pulling her head back, exposing her neck as much as possible in the cramped space.

"Is that why you've been half delirious and exhausted all day? Because your mother locked you in the closet last night? For not having sex with me yesterday—*the day we met?*"

Trapped and stretched out like a feast on my lap, Aurora trembles from head to toe and aims vulnerable green eyes at me. The defiant set of her features slices me in two.

"You were never going to tell me either, were you?" I snarl.

"You didn't need to know! I can—"

I release her arms and grip her jaw, framing her face with my massive hand.

"No, I don't want to hear your excuses, Aurora. You're mine now. Only mine. No one except for me, not even your mother, will ever hurt you again."

A single tear escapes her lashes and trails along my finger.

"We're leaving. You're moving into the townhouse with me and never coming back here again," I snarl.

Her glare hardens my cock and awakens my need to conquer and claim every inch of her.

"No. I'm staying at my parents'," she insists.

"Why? Does she lock your brother in the closet, too?"

"She'd do that and so much worse if I left. I need to stay."

"We'll take him with us," I snarl, half delirious from her ass against my thighs and beyond furious over how she was suffering in silence *because of me*.

"Are you stupid? He's the heir to the Achilles family. You may be the Vivaldi heir, but you can't kidnap him without starting a citywide war. Thousands of people would die in the crossfire."

How in the hell is this tiny woman so smart, scrappy, and stubborn?

"Then thousands die. I don't care. You're my only priority, *mia topolina*."

She scoffs and shoves against my chest.

"So much for being a man of your word. Let me go."

"Excuse me?"

She stills as the menace in my tone registers, but the anger vibrating from her fills the car as she speaks with barely leashed fury.

"You're lying. I'm not your only priority. Your sisters and parents are important, too. Can you imagine how hurt Serenity would be if she heard you kidnapped an eight-year-old boy and put everyone associated with your family in danger?"

I grind my teeth and fight the urge to tilt my hips. The heat emanating from the juncture of her thighs scrambles my thoughts while her helplessness against my strength heightens my desire.

"If you don't want to see how much of a monster I can be, you'd better start giving me options, *topolina*, because right now all I can hear is you telling me no."

"I just need some time to figure things out."

"You don't have time. You're not going back into that house until I can protect you."

"I've lived there my entire life. I'll be fine."

"You've only been my betrothed for one day, and it landed you in the fucking closet. You're not going in until I know you're safe."

"My mom won't take away my phone if she knows you'll call, so tell me you can't wait to hear my voice later or something stupid like that, but make sure she hears you. It'll probably be enough for her to leave me alone."

As my rage boils within my veins, I realize there's only one way I can appease her mother without hurting Aurora.

I lean forward and nip her ear.

"Put your hands behind your back," I snarl.

"What? Why?"

"If you touch me, I'll take you right here, right now, in the driver's seat of my car while

193

parked in front of your parents' house in broad daylight. Do you think she's watching through the windows? Is fucking you the only way to solve this?"

She shakes her head but doesn't release the front of my shirt.

"Move your hands, *mia topolina*. Now," I growl.

She does, which pushes her breasts against her shirt as though in offering. My mouth waters.

I feast, licking, nipping, and sucking her ear, throat, and lips, until she gasps and writhes in my lap.

It's too much but not enough. I need more.

Her whimper as I unbutton the front of her dress arrows straight to my balls, but I pull the fabric away from her shoulder and close my mouth over her pale flesh. She gasps and rolls her hips. The friction almost sends me over the edge.

I twist my fingers in her hair, holding her where I want her, and cup her breast through her clothes as I bite down harder on her shoulder. Her nipple stiffens and presses against my palm. I flick my thumb over the sensitive peak and enjoy her moan as I skim my hand down her side. She squirms as I slip my hand under her dress, but with her knees stretched wide around my hips, she's powerless to stop me as I find her clit through her panties.

I growl and lick the flesh trapped within my mouth. She's soaked. Wetness coats my fingertips even through the fabric.

I stroke her with my thumb. She squeaks and clenches her knees around me. I shift my hand, wedge my fingers between us, and draw a slow circle over her entire sex.

The scent of her desire fills the vehicle. My mouth waters and lust muddles my mind. I yank my hand free only to dive into the thin scrap of material blocking me from her pussy.

Her breathy sound of alarm mingles with my groan as I sink my middle finger into her tight, wet heat. My control slips and fire rushes down my shaft to wet my pants.

I growl, release my bite, and nip a line up her neck to murmur against her jugular.

"*Mio Dio*, you're soaked. You're going to cum all over my hand, aren't you, *mia topolina*?"

She squeaks and shakes her head. I chuckle and lick her ear.

"Yes, you will. This one's for me, *capisci?*" She shakes her head harder. I curl my finger inside her and groan. "I need to see you fly apart in my arms. Give me your pleasure, Aurora. Let me see you at your most vulnerable."

Her breath hitches. I angle my thumb and stroke her clit as I surge my finger in and out of her pussy. She makes adorable and enticing sounds of distress as I work her higher and higher. I suction my mouth high on her neck, just under her jawline, and growl in delight as she undulates in my lap.

Her thighs clench a millisecond before her pussy flutters around my finger.

It's not enough. I sink my digit knuckle-deep and stroke her G-spot over and over.

She screams and erupts. I lift my head and relish the sight of her locked in rapture as she floods my hand with her honey.

She's the most erotic sight I've ever seen.

I gentle my touch and wait until she recovers enough to meet my gaze before I slip my finger out of her pussy. Her throaty moan spears through my hard as steel erection, but I torture myself further by sticking my finger in my mouth and sucking her juices off.

Her flavor bursts through my tastebuds. I close my eyes and savor every lick as I clean my digits, and when I lift my lids again, her glazed eyes almost push me too far.

I snarl and cover her pussy with her panties before lifting her off my lap to put her back in her seat, but she pulls her arms from behind her back and clutches my shoulders.

"W-wait. You can't go in there with a hard on. She—"

"No."

I can't force myself to say more. If she touches me, I'll fuck her. The only way I will not be balls deep inside her pussy is if I completely ignore my cock.

I guide her over the console, careful to protect her head, and settle her in her seat.

After snatching half a dozen tissues from the glove box and giving her a few, I brace my forearm on the wheel and lean my head on top. I wipe a spot on my thigh and pretend to clean up after an impromptu quickie in case we have prying eyes.

A sour taste infects my mouth, tarnishing my bride-to-be's lingering flavor.

As deplorable as it was of me to maul her in the car, I would have taken it much further if Aurora wasn't so important to me.

I can't believe I'm going to let her waltz back into her familial home as though nothing is amiss, but we're both boxed in by our roles in life, and I've done everything within my power to protect her, at least for tonight.

No matter what it takes, I'll free both her and her brother, because even though I haven't seen him since he was a toddler, if Tristan is important to Aurora, he's important to me.

The feisty, wickedly smart mafia princess has stolen my heart and made herself the center of my universe.

I'll do anything for her.

Including kidnap her brother if she can't find another way to protect him from their abusive mother.

CHAPTER 13

Aurora Achilles

MY LEGS WOBBLE, and if it weren't for Giorgio's arm around me, I'd tumble down the stairs, but he pulls me tighter against his side and smirks down at me.

He's going to kill me. No amount of porn or research could've prepared me for what he just did to me. I didn't know I could have a full body orgasm like that.

He was only using his finger, too. One finger. I'll never survive the monster hanging between his legs.

The front door opens before we reach the top step. A breeze carries my mother's cloying perfume to me. The residual glow from my orgasm fades and reality crashes onto my head.

My insufficiencies emanate from my mother's eyes, and I become acutely aware of how horrible I must look.

Mussed hair. Unbuttoned top. Smelling of sex. Hickeys all over my neck and shoulder. Giorgio didn't even give me a chance to freshen up.

As my mother offers him her signature smile, I realize he did it on purpose.

Gratitude, annoyance, and sadness spear through me.

"We didn't expect you so early," my mother says to me after greeting Giorgio.

When she reaches for my shoulders to give me the stereotypical kiss on each cheek Italian mothers usually give their children, Giorgio shifts me away, putting his body between us.

"Forgive me, Madona. I'm not quite ready to let go of her just yet. Maybe after a cup of coffee?"

Oh. My. God.

The nerve of this man.

"Of course! You're always welcome to visit. Horatio is currently in a meeting, but he should be out soon," my mother says.

She gestures for us to follow her into the house. Giorgio pulls me along beside him, giving me no option to balk.

I wouldn't dare, anyway. He stole the strength from my legs when he wrenched that orgasm from my body.

My mother leads us into the sitting room and requests some coffee and snacks from the nearest staff. He rushes to comply.

Before Giorgio can pull me down onto the loveseat beside him, my father's voice echoes down the hall. A group of six or seven men walk past the doorway as he ushers them to the foyer.

Ice slides down my spine as I recognize my father's consigliere's voice. It's cowardly, but I lean into my future husband and grab the back of his shirt. He flicks unreadable dark brown eyes down at me, but returns his attention to my mother, maintaining his show for my sake.

We remain standing until my father steps into the room.

"Giorgio! What a pleasant surprise," he says.

Otello Tempe, my father's right-hand man and closest confidant, saunters in with the smooth walk of a man who believes he can do no wrong. My skin crawls. The air turns frigid as hatred and lies fill the room.

I twist my fingers in Giorgio's shirt before I regain control of myself and force myself to relax.

My mother ensures I don't see Otello very often, so even though he lives on the third floor, we rarely see each other face-to-face.

It's been at least six months since I was in the same room with him, but he looks the same, except for the cut of his suit and the color of his tie.

"I'm sure you've met before, but it may have been a few years, so let me introduce you again. Giorgio Vivaldi, meet Otello Tempe, my brother and consigliere."

The ice infecting my bones spreads outward until my skin turns clammy.

I hate when my father introduces him as a blood relative. He's not. The man single-handed tore my family apart behind my father's back.

The worst part is my father remains completely clueless.

I abhor him, but I can't choose who my father works with. Or fucks.

They don't keep it a secret within these walls, but outside of the house, they seem no closer than the brothers my father proclaims them to be.

I silently thank Giorgio as he pulls the same stunt with my so-called uncle as he did with my mother, keeping his body between mine and the new arrival's.

As my partner in crime navigates the conversation with eerie ease, I act as though I don't even exist, completely fine with fading into the background.

Until Otello pulls me into the discussion.

"I knew you two would get along, but it's still a relief to see things going so well," he says.

"Ah, well, who wouldn't get along with Aurora? She's an angel."

My heart skips a beat at Giorgio's unexpected praise and thinly veiled threat. While I appreciate him staking a claim over me, the less said about us in our current company, the better.

I feign happiness as best I can but hope he reads my reluctance to continue the conversation in the tightness of my smile.

"She wasn't always so well behaved, or so low maintenance, so it's nice your union is off to a great start."

All the blood drains from my face. My head spins. Giorgio's fingers flex into my side.

"I'm sorry you had doubts." His flat tone sends a shiver down my spine. "I can't stay long, so you'll have to excuse me." He turns to my mother and gives a slight dip of his chin. "Thank you for the warm welcome."

He pulls me into the hall without another word or backward glance. My legs tingle with numbness, but I force one in front of the other, eager to put more distance between myself and all three of the people in my parents' sitting room.

"Which one is your room?" Giorgio asks, snapping me out of my spiral.

I take a deep breath and blink until my surroundings come into focus.

"Tristan's room." I point to the first room on the left. "My room." The second on the left. "My mother's suite." The last door on the right. "My father's suite." The first door on the right.

Giorgio's alertness surpasses the level he showed when we visited his lawyer's office. He scans the ceiling for cameras and studies the paintings and fixtures for abnormalities. His eyes pause on both mine and my brother's doorhandles.

A wave of uncertainty grips me as I realize the sexiest, most ruthless man I've ever met is about to see my room. He'll be the first male to step foot in my personal domain in six years. That's counting Tristan's last visit. My father rarely haunts the hall, electing to sleep either in his study or on the third floor.

Otello never steps foot beyond the second-floor landing.

Deciding to act before I lose my courage, I pull away from Giorgio, surprised when he lets me, and grab his hand. After weaving my fingers within his, I pull him toward my room and fling open the door.

Like a character in a comic book, I rush headlong through the doorway only to screech to a halt halfway across the room. After taking a few calming breaths, I turn to see his reaction.

It's shocking how expressive the man can be. Without a single word, he eases all my fears. Even though the menace never leaves his aura, the upward tilt of his lips and the interest shining in his eyes assures me he likes my room.

Shit. My prescription sits on the top shelf.

I tug him into the bathroom and pray he didn't see it.

"Can you give me a minute? I'll open the door when I'm done."

He quirks a brow.

"Don't women usually hide *in* the bathroom when they need a minute?"

"Look, you can go through the cabinets in here while you wait, if you want. Just let me tidy up in the bedroom a little."

He encloses me in his arms and cups the back of my head in his massive hand.

"If you're trying to hide naughty toys, don't bother. They'll just become tools in my arsenal, anyway. I'll learn how to use your favorites and watch you writhe on my cock as I torture and tease you."

"You don't need any help." His eyes flash with masculine pride as I stroke his ego with my words and throaty response. "I don't have toys, but..." I take a deep breath and reveal my insecurities. "I've never had a guy in my room before. Never had anyone in my room besides my mother. I just want to tidy it up a bit. Please?"

He groans and takes my mouth in a searing, desperate kiss. When he pulls away, we both gasp for breath.

"What are you doing to me, *topolina*?" he murmurs with his forehead pressed against mine.

I don't have an answer for him, so I say nothing.

"Fine, but I'm opening the door in two minutes if you haven't already."

"Thank you," I say before pecking his cheek and closing the door between us.

Despite the urge to grab my medicine first, I open my bedside table and drop the jar of odds and ends—including my bobby pins—into the back of the drawer. I take my medicine from the top shelf and slip it into my purse, moving carefully so the pills don't clatter, and zip it closed before rushing to my desk and moving things around.

The bathroom door opens not even thirty seconds later.

He catches me before I can rush into my walk-in closet.

"Is this where your mother locks you in?" he asks, but he already knows the answer before I shake my head, since there's no lock on the door. Not even the bathroom has a lock.

"But she locks your bedroom door?"

I nod.

"It doesn't bother you?"

I shrug.

He stalks to the door and studies the old-fashioned handle. His face hardens as he realizes there's no way to lock or unlock it—from either side—without the key.

Without a word, he moves on to my vanity. Then my bookshelf. Then my desk.

My heart pounds against my sternum as he squats to look under and behind my workspace.

"What are you looking for?" I ask.

"I thought you'd have a much more elaborate setup," he says.

"My computer?" I clarify.

He nods. I scoff and cross my arms over my chest, but stop myself before I say something stupid or revealing.

"This is more than enough," I compromise.

He doesn't need to know I could hack into the FBI database from a burner phone. The feds would kick in my door less than thirty seconds later without the protection of an IP mask, but I'd still have the classified information he wanted.

He retraces his steps to my bookshelf.

"What are you studying in college?"

I hesitate too long. He swings narrowed eyes my way.

"Can we talk about this later?"

I shift my gaze to the door. He relents and turns to face my bed.

Heat flames in my cheeks as I realize looking at the door and reminding him of my parents' proximity won't stop him from laying me out on my comforter and continuing where we left off in the car. Lust shimmers in my veins.

His wicked smile fans the flames of my desire. An inferno burns in my core.

He stalks toward me, grabs me by the throat, and pulls me against him.

"If I were a nicer man, I'd leave without touching you, but I need you to think of me every time you walk into this room. Every time you sit at this desk. Every time you lie in your bed," he growls against my temple.

Shivers wrack my spine.

"I need to be the center of your world." He nips my sensitive ear. "Because you're already the center of mine."

My heart melts. I can't deny him, even though the thought of losing my virginity in this room curdles my stomach.

"Put your hands behind your back," he snarls.

Every cell in my body turns to mush. I comply without a thought.

"*Mio Dio*, you're perfect."

He kisses me like a man possessed. His hands touch me everywhere, framing my face, tangling in my hair, gripping my neck, and skimming my shoulders.

He hooks his forearm under my ass and lifts me off my feet. I wrap my legs around his waist and grab his nape on reflex.

"Bad girl," he hisses against my lips.

I squeak as he kicks my desk chair out of the way and pushes my keyboard to the side before setting me on the desk. The cool surface seeps through my skirt and panties, shocking my overheated pussy.

He drops to his knees, pushes my knees apart, and pins my calves to the front of my desk.

"What are you—?"

Fireworks burst in my skull as he seals his mouth over my entire sex. Even with my panties muffling the sensation, I gasp and mindlessly tug his hair as he licks and nips me through the fabric.

Pressure builds in my core. I whine when he pulls away.

He scoops me up and drops me onto my bed. My grunt of surprise morphs to a moan as his mouth closes over my left breast. His weight pins my lower half to the bed, otherwise I'd jackknife onto the floor when he pinches my nipple between his teeth.

It stings even with my dress and bra between us.

He lifts his head.

"Pull my hair harder, *mia topolina*. Make it hurt. I deserve it for what I'm about to do to you."

I tug his hair and writhe as he frames my breasts with his gigantic hands, highlighting our size differences.

He closes his mouth over my right breast.

Mio Dio, I never knew my nipples could be so sensitive.

He disappears. I blink up at my ceiling in confusion. My entire body throbs with need. It hurts. I don't like it.

"Stay in here until your brother comes home. I'll text you when I get to the car. Show it to your mother if she gives you trouble. I'll see you first thing in the morning. *Capisci?*"

He leaves the room without waiting for an answer. I stare blindly at the ceiling for long, unending moments, not moving even when my phone chimes in my purse, until the worst of my frustration passes.

After responding to Giorgio's text, I drop my phone on the bed and drag myself into the shower. When I meet my eyes in the mirror, my heart lurches.

My eyes shine brighter than ever before. Faint bruises form on my neck, but Giorgio's teeth marks still ring the dark purple bruise on my shoulder. I shiver and wipe away my tears, not even sure why I feel the need to cry, and slather on makeup.

When I step into the hall, silence drifts up the stairs, so I wait in the foyer until the SUV pulls up.

Tristan's animated retelling of the day soothes my aching heart, but by the time I say goodnight to him, I realize my brother can't stop the slow bleeding caused by Giorgio's infiltration.

I take my medicine from my purse, settle at my desk, and open the college coursework my mother expects to see on my screen before staring blankly at the wall.

The door opens. My mother's icy gaze wipes away whatever lust lingers from Giorgio's visit. She watches me swallow my handful of pills before locking the door without a word.

I slump. Breathe in. Breathe out. Straighten my spine. Roll my neck. Crack my knuckles. Then dive in to catch up on what I missed last night.

First thing on my list: send an anonymous tip to Nico. Serenity's tablet didn't malfunction; someone hid malware in a look-alike app, and they would have gotten away with it if she hadn't had automatic updates permitted. I flushed the device and added some code to increase her security and prevent the hackers from obtaining whatever information they hoped to glean.

I continue down my mental list, checking my parents' devices, looking into the people I met and the names I learned today, completing a handful of jobs, and finishing a few assignments before sitting back in my chair and sighing.

As I start a deep dive into Giorgio's assets, my mouth dries. All the funds I've stashed away over the years seem puny compared to his wealth. I don't understand why he gave me everything in the prenuptial agreement, but I don't want it. Even though his businesses and properties seem surprisingly clean, they're still mafia adjacent.

None of my efforts matter if I can't protect Tristan from my fucked up family. All those years of studying and working mean nothing if I can't get him out of my parents' clutches.

As I run through potential options—tossing most of them in the trash heap before they even form—I fiddle with my mouse.

When a semi-decent idea pops into the forefront of my mind, I focus my eyes only to freeze when I realize what I absently pulled up while brainstorming.

Many, many years ago, I collected DNA samples from everyone in my family and sent them for tests.

My brother's results sit on the left side of the screen. Otello Tempe's show on the left.

They're a match. The 99.9 on the paternity test bores into my brain.

I exit out of both screens with shaky fingers and delete my history.

My father isn't Tristan's father. Otello is.

Technically, I'm the Achilles heir, but the mafia is too patriarchal. No one would accept me when Tristan is around, and there's no way in hell I'll ever reveal the truth and put my brother in danger.

The worst part?

I think Otello Tempe, my father's consigliere and lover, knows he's the one who put Tristan into my mother's womb.

CHAPTER 14

Giorgio Vivaldi

I PUSH THROUGH THE PAIN and continue past my original set count, hunkering deeper into my stance and lowering my center as I put more power behind my extra punches. Fiero grunts and leans into the bag, my unexpected swings almost knocking him off balance. When I finally step back and shake out my arms, he sighs and rolls his shoulders.

"Will breaking the bag make you feel better?" Fiero asks with more snark than common sense.

"You're lucky I didn't beat on your sorry ass instead," I snarl.

"What's got your tits in a tangle this morning?" he asks.

I catch the hand towel he tosses at me and wipe the sweat from my face.

"Nico Russo thinks the *stronzos* threatening our families have shifted to online attacks. Stealing information and planting bugs without even leaving their fucking hideout," I snarl.

When I grab the shin pads and throw them at him, he groans. I roll my eyes and include the bigger kick pad while mumbling about weak-ass bitches who chose the wrong career path if they can't handle a few blows with protection.

"Did they attack his business or his home?" Fiero asks as he straps his last shin guard onto his leg and stands.

"Both, but his team is so busy with cleaning up the mess, they can't find the source."

I stalk across the mat to Fiero. He curses and pivots just in time to accept my kick on his shin pads instead of the side of his legs.

"Fuck, are you trying to kill me?"

"You won't die, not from this," I promise.

"Oh, there's a relief."

I land a flurry of kicks, interrupting the conversation as he focuses on protecting himself. When my thighs burn and calves cramp, I stalk around the mats, working out the kinks, before moving to the center again.

"Don't you want to hear what I found on Aurora?" he asks.

"No," I snarl and strike.

He curses and fields my volley of random combinations.

"Why?" he grunts.

I finish with a push kick, shoving my sole into the shield pad so hard Fiero stumbles back several steps.

"I know enough already. She'll tell me the rest when she's ready."

"Are you sure about that?"

"Yes."

"Then tell her about the cyberattacks on Nico Russo."

I drop the hand towel without using it and turn to face him.

"Ask for her help," he says with a shrug before dropping to unstrap the pads from his shins.

"Why? What did you find?"

He lifts his head and meets my eyes as he unhooks the Velcro behind his left calf.

"She's a few credits away from earning her bachelor's degree in computer science, and according to her professors, she's a genius. She has the highest grades in all her classes."

He stands with the pads tucked under one arm and saunters to the cleaning station.

"She's only eighteen. She just graduated from high school," I snarl.

I might strangle the man as he sanitizes the pads with nonchalance emanating from his every move.

"She locked her records and delayed her diploma, but she graduated years ago."

I curse and stomp to the locker room, angry I let Fiero goad me into asking about Aurora behind her back. As the hot shower beats down on my shoulders, I pray my early morning workout is enough to help me maintain control throughout the day, but when my cock half hardens at the mere thought of kissing Aurora, I hiss and smack the shower controls.

Freezing water shocks me into the present and cools my ardor.

"There's more," Fiero says from the stall beside me.

I turn off the shower and yank the curtain open. When I don't respond, electing to towel dry in silence, he takes the hint and changes the subject.

"I looked into her family situation, too."

I hang my towel on the hook and reach for my lotion.

"Did you know her father's consigliere claims the Achilles family home as his place of residency?"

I pause mid-smear with my foot propped up on the bench. Most consiglieres have their own homes. My uncle has his own townhouse, despite spending most of his time at our family residence.

"And I can't find any apartments or condos under his name, either."

I grunt and finish lotioning my entire body.

"Are you trying to tell me he lives with the Achilles family?" I snarl.

I didn't get that vibe from Aurora. Her reaction made it seem like she hadn't expected to see him. Like it had been a while since he visited.

"He's seen going in and out of hotels and apartments, but I'm not sure he's ever slept in one place for more than a night or two at a time," Fiero says before turning off his shower.

"So, he's a man whore?" I scoff.

His towel muffles his reply.

"I think that's fair to say."

I pull on my clothes and toss my dirties in my duffle before checking the time on my phone.

"Don't call or text me today unless it's an emergency." I shove my phone in my pocket and head for the door. "And stay away from the townhouse," I demand.

"Got it, boss. Go get your lady before you break all the gym equipment." As the locker door closes behind me, his last words pull a tight smirk from me. "Goddamn beast might break my legs tomorrow if he doesn't get what he wants."

HEARTLESS VOWS

I hop in my car and head straight to the Achilles family home. As the first rays of light brighten the sky, I pull into the driveway behind a black SUV. A man older than my father stands beside the open back passenger door. He looks vaguely familiar. His sweater and slacks label him as an educator, but I hate to judge a book by its cover, so I hold my judgment until he meets my gaze.

His friendly smile, intelligence, and manners clear away my suspicion.

The side door of the house opens and Aurora steps out. Her smile steals my breath. I want her to greet me like that, but she has yet to notice me. Locked in a playful conversation with the boy who trails out after her, she laughs and throws her arm over his shoulder as they walk down the sidewalk.

Tristan. Her brother. The heir to the Achilles family and the only reason I can't have Aurora underneath me all night long.

The last time I saw him, he was knee height. Now the top of his head reaches Aurora's chin.

When Aurora notices me, excitement brightens her expression before she catches herself. Worry and uncertainty dampen her joy, but she still offers me a tight smile before turning to the old man.

"Good morning, Mr. Hearthright. Please excuse us for a moment, then Tristan is all yours for the day," Aurora says.

Mr. Hearthright agrees with reserved amusement.

A surge of nervous energy works up from my toes, the sensation so foreign I take an embarrassing amount of time to recognize it before I shove it away.

Aurora guides Tristan over to stand in front of me. As she introduces us, Tristan sizes me up. I do the same to him, aware of just how brutally honest young boys can be.

He's a smaller, masculine version of Aurora, so I can't find much fault in him. He still carries the round face and innocence of youth, but even at first glance, it's obvious he's related to Aurora. If she were a little older, I'd think she was his mom, but only at first glance.

When he sticks out his hand for a shake, I take it and enjoy the firm squeeze he gives me.

He drops his friendly expression and sends me what must be all the consternation in his tiny body.

"I may be only eight years old, but if you ever hurt her, I'll kill you."

Aurora gasps and clasps her hand over his mouth before trying to tug him away.

I don't let go. She hisses my name.

"He didn't mean it. Don't—"

I lean down to his eye level.

"Do you know how to use a gun?"

He peels Aurora's hand off his mouth.

"Yes, but my sister won't even let me touch one. Don't worry, though, I can still kill you."

"And how would you do that?" I ask.

"Maybe a knife. Or a car. A truck might be better, since you're so big. Poison could work, too. Or—"

"Tristan, stop!" Aurora pleads.

I drop into a squat and pull him closer.

"All good options, if you know what you're doing. No skill is a wasted skill if it can protect the ones you love. I can teach you, if you want?"

Aurora hisses my name again, but a smile spreads across Tristan's face.

"Promise?" he asks.

"Promise. We'll protect Aurora together," I vow.

"Shake on it?" he half-asks, half-demands.

"Of course," I respond.

He gives my hand a firm shake. I try not to crush his tiny digits but reciprocate with enough force he knows I'm serious.

Aurora throws her hands up in the air and turns to Mr. Hearthright with bewilderment on her face. He shrugs as if to say it's none of his business, but the amused tilt of his lips shows his approval.

I remember where I've seen him before. He chaperoned a group of mafia elite children to specialty summer camps over a decade ago.

Aurora must have chosen him for his expertise. I silently approve of her selection. He'll keep Tristan safe, no matter what threats they face throughout the day. My respect for him grows when he greets Tristan with the same respect he showed me.

As Aurora says goodbye to Tristan with an extra admonishment and a warning to behave, longing lodges within my throat and constructs my airway. I yearn to watch Aurora care for our children with such love, but the concept feels a bit too abstract and far away, so the thought of being included in their rote morning activities fills me with a stronger sense of envy.

She shuts the door and waves as the SUV drives away. Long after it disappears from view, she keeps her back to me. I use the time to sort through my emotions and tuck them away for later before focusing on the next endeavor.

This one will be much more carnal. Nothing will stop me from enjoying every inch of my bride-to-be. After today, she'll be Aurora Vivaldi in every way except name.

Maybe we shouldn't wait a full four months to make it official. We signed prenups without our parents' knowledge. What's stopping us from going down to the courthouse and signing other documents?

I dismiss the idea. Aurora deserves the most lavish wedding in the history of New York City.

The fury on her face when she turns to me is not the expression I expect.

"Do you need anything from inside the house?" I ask before she speaks.

She closes her mouth and sets her lips in a mutinous line as she shakes her head. I open the passenger door and offer to help her inside, but when she refuses and tries to avoid touching me, I grab her and pin her against the back door with my bulk.

Her silky hair and soft lips prove too tempting. I weave my digits into her locks and kiss her with bruising force, but I need her too much to hold back. After a moment of shock, she gives as fiercely as she gets, grabbing my waist and digging her nails into my flesh through my shirt. Her anger merges with desperation, pulling a groan from my chest. My cock tests the strength of my trouser seams and need draws my balls up close to my body.

I pull away with a curse, yank her hands off me, grab her by the nape, and push her into her seat, protecting her head from hitting the doorframe by covering it with my arm.

Her wide eyes feed my hunger as I close the door. I stalk around the hood, wedge myself behind the wheel, and pull out of the driveway before we have a truly X-rated moment in front of her familial home.

She adjusts the air control dial, aims her vents at her face, leans back, and closes her eyes. I settle my hand on her thigh. She stiffens and directs a glare at my face.

"Do you know how hard I've worked to keep Tristan away from all that shit? How could you offer to teach him how to *kill* people? He's eight! He'll take you seriously!"

"I *was* serious."

"No. You can't. I don't want you to."

I snuff my initial response after a glance at her expression. When I reach for her hand, she moves it away, but I lean further and grab her wrist.

"I know you want to protect him. I do, too."

"No, you just want to corrupt him," she snaps.

"How long do you think he'll survive as a mafia kingpin without what I can teach him?"

She presses her other hand to her eyes and takes a deep breath through gritted teeth.

"I graduated from high school early, earned an associate's degree in business management, am a semester away from earning my bachelor's in computer science, and make almost a million dollars online annually."

Heavy silence fills the car as I process her words.

I wish I could tell her how proud and in awe I am of her, but the topic jump fills me with foreboding.

"Why? Why have you pushed yourself so hard for so long?"

I already know, but I need to hear her say it.

"I was going to run away with him. I'd buy us both new identities and hide somewhere far, far away from my family. We'd escape the mafia and live a long, carefree life without all the danger."

"When were you planning to disappear on me?" I snarl.

"What? No, I can't go anymore. When my mother told me I was getting married, I knew I'd fucked up by waiting too long. I can't leave, but maybe I can still find somewhere safe for Tristan."

I pull over before I cause an accident and throw the car into park before moving both hands to the wheel, afraid I'll hurt Aurora if I touch her right now.

"Why are you telling me this now?" I growl.

"Because I can't make it make sense anymore!"

The agony in her voice reveals more than I can dissect, but her wild eyes, pale face, and rapid, shallow breaths suggest she's on the verge of a mental breakdown.

Only one thing could bring her to such depths.

"You can't send him away, can you?"

My gravelly baritone ruins my attempt at delivering the news gently, but instead of breaking, she turns haunted eyes to mine.

"I'm a selfish coward, aren't I? I should let him go, but I need him in my life. I just can't figure out how to keep him safe."

"Are you asking for my help?"

"I... I don't think I can do this alone anymore, but..."

"But you think I'll turn him into a monster?"

She sighs and drops her face into her hands.

"He can't become my father," she mumbles.

Her answer isn't what I expect, but it doesn't surprise me. I peel my fingers off the steering wheel and gather her to me with as much gentleness as I can muster. She drops her hands into her lap. I cup the back of her head and frame the side of her face before forcing her teary eyes up to mine.

"He has a solid, loving foundation because of you, Aurora. No matter what I teach him, he'll still be the Tristan you know and love. He will *always* regard you as the most important person in his life, at least until he starts his own family, and then he'll still welcome you into his home with open arms."

"How can you say that? You only saw him for two seconds."

"Two seconds is all I needed. He needs you the same way you need him. That's why you can't send him away, Aurora. Not because you're selfish, but because he still needs you. You recognized it, even if you couldn't put it into words."

"I don't know what to do anymore," she whispers.

The first tear escapes from her lashes and trails along my hand. I tuck my thumb under her chin and pull her closer to my face.

"Let me protect him the best way I know how. Let me teach him. The things I do may not always be legal, but I have my own morals, Aurora. He'll still be the Tristan you raised with love; he'll just also have the skills to survive the cutthroat, cruel world we live in."

"How can you promise me something like that? You can't—"

"I can and I will. Haven't I proven I'm a man of my word?"

She takes a shuddering breath and searches my expression. When she closes her eyes and nuzzles against my hand, my heart melts.

"You have." She filets me alive when she aims her shimmery emerald orbs at me. "I trust you, Giorgio."

"*Mio Dio*, didn't I warn you about saying my name?"

Her pupils shrink.

Despite the urgency pulsing through me, I take her mouth in a long, drugging kiss, and when I pull back, her swollen lips and dazed eyes fill me with pride and longing. She shifts in her seat, rubbing her thighs together and pressing her breasts against her shirt. My cock pounds at the agony of being denied.

"Stay just like this, all soft and desperate for me, until I get us home. Are you wet already, *mia topolina*?"

When she mindlessly nods, I growl and dive back into her mouth, but pull back when lust threatens to break the dam of my control.

I wipe her tears off her face and steal a lick of the corner of her mouth, enjoying her gasp of surprise before settling my hand on her knee and pulling out into traffic.

After a few moments, she wiggles in her seat. I smirk and give her a warning out of the corner of my eye. She stills and gnaws on her bottom lip.

I slip my hand higher on her thigh. Her blush deepens. I change lanes and squeeze her leg. Her breath hitches.

With every change, I move my hand higher on her leg. When I turn onto the last street, I brush my pinky over her panties.

She smothers her gasp with her hand and grabs my wrist.

I snarl, expecting her to push me away, but groan when she parts her knees and guides my hand to her sex.

She's soaked.

I almost miss the driveway, but I slow just in time to mash the button for the gate and whip onto the property. As the gate closes behind us and the garage opens in front of us, I curl my fingers into her folds until her panties prevent me from going any deeper. She groans and tilts her hips as I flatten her clit with my palm.

I pull into the garage, turn off the car, and hit the button to close the door. Pain streaks through my groin as my trouser seam pinches my hard cock. I flex my fingers against her pussy and grind the heel of my palm in a circle over her clit.

My seat belt buckle clacks against the window as I whip it out of the way. I unbuckle her and lean over the console to devour her mouth. She whimpers and kisses me with abandon.

I snarl and pull back.

"You're drenched and desperate for my cock, aren't you, *mia topolina?*"

She whines and nods.

"You want to cum on my hand again?"

She nods and tilts her chin as though asking for another kiss.

"Use your words, Aurora. Tell me what you want."

She hooks her arm around my nape and dares me to pull away, knowing I couldn't if I tried, and I sure as hell don't want to.

"Everything. I want everything. If it's with you, I want it," she says.

The honesty and vulnerability shining from her eyes steal my breath. She becomes the foundation of my soul. I'm nothing without her.

No more waiting. She's ready.

Aurora Achilles is mine.

All mine.

CHAPTER 15

Aurora Achilles

IT'S TOO MUCH BUT NOT ENOUGH. I need more. Every ounce of unsatisfied lust from yesterday roars through me, increasing my desperation and heightening my senses.

"Take out my cock," Giorgio demands.

My fingers tremble from the force of my need, but he encourages and rewards me with teasing strokes of his fingers as I unfasten his belt and work the front of his trousers open.

My clit pulses and wetness seeps through my panties.

I reach into his pants and pull out his hot, hard cock. Awe and apprehension spear through me. He's too big, but I want him. Only him.

"Kneel in the seat and take me into your mouth," he growls.

I whine and wriggle against his fingers.

He snarls, grabs my hips, lifts me onto my knees, pulls my upper half over the console, and holds me down by my nape before yanking my panties down and swatting my ass. I gasp at the sting only to moan as he rubs his big, warm hand over the spot until the pain morphs into pleasure and settles between my legs.

He teases his fingertips over the curve of my ass and the back of my thigh, *oh so close* to my pussy but nowhere near where I need him.

"C'mon, *mia topolina*, don't you want to taste me again? Open your mouth."

His tip bobs against my chin, leaving a smear of fragrant fluid behind. I sneak my tongue out and flick over the leaking slit. Despite the ocean of magma boiling in my core, indignation flares through me at the inequality of our positions, and words escape my mouth before I can think better of them.

"C'mon, my heartless jerk, don't you want me to cum on your hand again? *Touch me*."

He does. In one ruthless motion, he shoves my mouth down onto his cock and sinks two fingers into my pussy. I shriek at the unexpected yet wonderful stretch, but his thick girth flattens my tongue and invades my throat. Terror grips me, sharpening my senses and triggering my fight reflexes, but he lifts me by my hair and pulls his fingers out of my pussy. I cough and choke on my spit as he strokes over my clit with shocking accuracy. Pressure builds deep in my core. My thighs shake.

"Suck me, *mia topolina*. I'm already so close, but so are you, aren't you?"

His growl pebbles my nipples and fills me with yearning. I nod and swirl my tongue around his tip, wanting to please him but too apprehensive to take more of him into my mouth. When he strokes the length of his fingers through my folds, stimulating every millimeter of my pussy, and gentles his hand in my hair, I close my lips around him and adjust my balance to wrap a hand around his shaft.

He murmurs deep, guttural praises and dips a finger past my entrance while rubbing my clit.

I whine and wiggle my hips. He pushes down on the back of my head, but when I stiffen and shake my head, he releases my hair.

He groans and wraps his fist around mine at the base of his shaft. His hand covers so much, I won't choke if I take all that's left jutting from his grip.

The tension drains from my shoulders. I swirl my tongue around his tip, enjoying the salty tang of his precum, and give a slow, shallow bob of my head. He hisses and pushes his finger deeper into my body.

I gasp and dip lower, taking more of him into my mouth.

He works his finger in and out of me. I mimic his rhythm, teetering on the edge of orgasm and enamored by the bunching of his thighs. When he adds a second finger and pushes deeper than before, I whimper around his shaft. His veins pulse on my lips.

"Now, *mia topolina*," he growls. "Let go. Cum on my hand as you swallow every drop."

He twists his wrist and crooks his fingers inside me, hitting the sensitive spot at the front of my channel while rubbing his thumb over my clit.

I explode. He groans as his cock jerks in my mouth. Salty, sweet fluid spurts onto my tongue. I swallow and clench around his fingers as wave after wave of euphoria crashes over me.

He pulls my face up to his and devours my mouth, staking his claim and declaring his devotion with every impatient invasion of his tongue. I give him everything. My head spins. Sticky wetness coats my thighs. His thick fingers shift inside me.

A whine escapes my throat.

"Don't worry, *mia topolina*, I'm nowhere near done with you yet."

With breathtaking ease, he opens the driver's door and pulls me out after him. I don't know how he does it, but his fingers never leave my pussy as he gathers me to his chest and wraps my legs around his waist. His cock bobs against my ass, teasing in and out of my skirt with every step as he stalks into the townhouse.

I don't recall hearing the car door shut and don't know where my panties are, but I lose the will to care as he shoulders the door to the living room open.

Peace settles over me as the unique ambiance of the house infiltrates my senses until Giorgio commands my full attention by pressing my back against the wall and dominating my mouth. With teeth and tongue, he scrambles my mind and reawakens my urgency.

I writhe and clutch at his shoulders as he curls his fingers inside me.

The world spins. He sits me on the armrest and leans me back on the couch. With my ass higher than my head, my skirt falls up my torso and all the blood rushes to my face. He wedges his shoulders between my knees and licks my clit. Lightning spears through me. It's too intense. Too close to pain. I don't think I like it.

He licks me again and thrusts his fingers in and out of me. I scream, arch, and fight for freedom.

After stepping out from between my knees and moving them to one side, he flings me over his shoulder—with his digits still lodged in my pussy—and carries me into the kitchen. I hiss as he lays me out on the cold counter, but he parts my legs in a reverse move from the one before, settles his hips between them and covers me with his bulk. He demands another kiss. Trapped between granite and hard muscles, I groan and grab his nape as our tongues duel.

He's wearing too many clothes. I wrench his collar apart. Buttons skitter over the counter and ping onto the floor. I pull again until the fabric parts and shove it off his shoulders.

The jerk still has another shirt underneath.

He mashes my clit with the palm of his hand and curls his fingers inside me as he grabs my breast. My blouse and bra muffle the sensation, but the strength in his hand scrambles my thoughts.

I work the bottom hem of his shirt up his torso and growl when his arms prevent me from lifting it higher.

He ends our kiss and pulls it over his head and off one arm, but leaves it hanging from his shoulder, refusing to remove his fingers from my depths. Tattoos cover his arms and torso. His cock stands tall and thick from his open trousers. My mouth waters with the need to taste and explore.

He growls, studies me with heavy-lidded eyes, and licks his lips.

"You gonna cum from just looking at me, Aurora?"

"Hmm? What?"

"Your pussy just clenched around my fingers. *Mio Dio*, there you go again. Unbutton your blouse and show me those tits. I need to taste them before I feel you squeeze my cock like this."

I can't deny him, not when his eyes worship me, so I slip the buttons free and slowly reveal more and more of my flesh.

He's right. I might orgasm just by watching him.

"Fucking hell, Aurora, you're too perfect. Cum on my fingers again while I've got you splayed out on the kitchen counter like a feast."

He works his fingers in and out of my body. I writhe until he pins my lower belly to the counter with his other hand and strokes his thumb over my clit.

I implode. My mind fragments. Wonderful pain spreads from my core outward until my entire body throbs in relief. Sweat trickles down my temple.

"Good girl. That was fucking perfect, *mia topolina*. Now show me those breasts."

His thick rumble sounds above, below, and inside me. He melts my bones. Heats my blood. Becomes my entire universe.

I pull my blouse out of my skirt waistband, unfasten the front closure of my bra, and push the fabrics off my shoulders. His low groan reawakens my desire.

I squeak as he slides his rock-hard forearm under me and lifts my shoulders off the granite.

"Mine."

I die a quadrillion beautiful deaths as he licks, sucks, and nibbles my breasts with hunger in every bite, until each touch streaks to my core and becomes too much. He snarls when I push against his shoulders.

"Please stop, Giorgio. It hurts."

He lifts his head and studies my face before a devilish smirk twists his swollen lips. I whimper when he pulls me off the counter, pressing our chests together and forcing his fingers deeper into my pussy as I wrap my legs around his waist.

My shirt and bra tangle together on my arms and trap my elbows to my sides as he carries me up the stairs and into the bedroom. Needy, helpless sounds escape my throat as he lays me on the bed and grabs my breast, pinning my upper half to the comforter. I jackknife as he brushes his thumbs over my nipple and clit in tandem. When he spreads his fingers inside me, I push at his shoulders and try to curl in on myself, but my shirt and his unyielding strength keep me right where he wants me.

"Let's get this pretty little pussy ready for my big cock, yeah?"

I instinctually shake my head, even though I want to give him everything.

My hair splays over the bed and sticks to my sweaty temples. He tweaks my nipple and drops his eyes to watch his two fingers disappear into my body. I moan and tilt my hips. He spreads his digits. My toes tingle. Fresh arousal coats his fingers. His cock brushes against my inner thigh. I whine.

He adds a third finger. I open my mouth, but no sound emerges. The stretching hurts so good.

Too much. Not enough.

His eyes darken and cheeks flush as his cock leaks on my leg. I strain as his knuckles stretch my entrance.

He pulls out and wraps his drenched fist around his cock. I watch in fascination as he strokes himself from root to tip, coating himself in my arousal.

My heart lurches into my throat as he fits his bulbous head to my entrance, but he groans and rubs his tip over my entire slit, bumping my clit and earning himself a gasp.

I clench my fists at my sides, desperate to touch him but too far gone for words.

After a few epic strokes of my clit with his tip, he presses the first half an inch of his cock into me.

My animalistic whine fills the air. He groans and wrenches the fabric off my arms.

"Fucking hell, I need your hands on me. Touch me. Scratch me. Bite me. Whatever you need, Aurora. I can't hold back anymore."

True to his word, he grabs my hips and surges into me.

Agony overrides my pleasure. I gouge his forearms with my nails and wedge my knees against his stomach, trying to push him away, but he's too strong. He pulls back before thrusting impossibly deeper into my body. I scratch, fight, and sob until he pushes my legs off his torso and drops forward to bracket my head with his hands. Surrounded and filled by him, I cry and writhe as he murmurs apologies and praises against my temple, ear, and throat.

When he takes my mouth with the same fervor he claims my pussy, every ounce of pain in my body morphs to pleasure. The sudden flip scrambles my response. I push and pull, scratch and caress, gasp and grunt, and bite and lick without rhyme or reason, desperate for so many things, I don't know what I'm asking for.

He gives me everything. Every inch of his cock. Every ounce of his power. Every orgasm my body can muster. Every drop of his release. Every piece of his soul.

Silent tears trail over my temples as his cock jerks inside me. He holds me close, as though I'm something precious, and murmurs sweet words into my hair.

In the most profound and intimate moment of my life, I realize there's only one word to encompass the way I feel for Giorgio Vivaldi.

Love. I love him.

The jerk *made* me fall in love with him. He gave me no choice. He gave me *everything*.

Guilt sweeps through me. I haven't given him anything. I've omitted so many things.

Two could destroy everything.

One isn't important right now. I've been healthy for years and show no symptoms, so my medical issues can wait.

Tristan cannot. He's in danger.

"What's wrong, *mia topolina*? Did I hurt you?" Giorgio asks as he strokes my hair back from my sweaty temple.

"No, you didn't. I just… I l—" the word gets stuck in my throat.

His pleasure-laden eyes soften further.

"It's okay, Aurora. I know. I love you, too."

His declaration stuns me into nodding, but I sob and shake my head when I realize how much is at stake.

"I *lied* to you!"

Surprise wipes the lazy joy from his eyes.

"But I don't want your money, or your empire, or to trap you, or anything like that. I lied to protect Tristan," I beg him to understand.

He quirks a brow and rubs his thumb over my cheekbone, still propped on his elbows with his cock lodged deep inside my body.

"What lie did you tell me?"

The menace in his tone sends a chill down my spine even as his invasion stretches and wakes dormant parts of me.

"It's not what I told you, but what I didn't tell you," I say.

He brushes my hair back from my face and tilts his hips, grinding our joined bodies against each other. I gasp as my overworked organs throb with a mix of pain and pleasure.

"What did you not tell me?" he asks.

"I'm the Achilles heir. Tristan's father is Otello Tempe, not Horatio Achilles, but—"

Giorgio covers my mouth with his palm and wraps his long, thick fingers around my face.

Panic grips me until I realize my ragged breaths blow over the back of his hand. I pull my nails out of his back and search his expression.

My heart quails at the coldness in his eyes, and my pleasure gives way to discomfort as he puts emotional distance between us. With our bodies still locked together, his impersonal expression hurts.

"How do you know? When did you find out, and who else knows?"

He shifts his hand, tightens his grip on my face, and lean closer.

"If you say anything other than those three answers, I'm walking away. I don't want to cross a line I can't uncross. *Capisci*, Aurora?"

I nod. He lifts his hand. I take a deep, shaky breath before answering.

"I ran DNA tests on my family about five years ago. I think Otello suspects Tristan is his, but I don't think he knows for sure."

"Where are the results?"

"Hidden and encrypted. I'm the only one who can read the files."

"Why'd you check for paternity?" he asks.

"I… My mom… I don't think it was consensual. I think my uncle is why she locks our doors at night."

"He lives with you?"

"On the third floor. Yesterday was the—"

All the air rushes from my lungs as he rises, taking his warmth and leaving me empty and alone.

"You're not going back into that house," he snarls as he stomps toward the bathroom. The play of his ass muscles as his trousers bunch underneath the firm globes and the bobbing of his drenched half-hard cock distract me, but warm wetness seeps from between my legs. I pull the corner of the comforter over me and glare at his back.

"My father will kill Tristan if he finds out. I can't leave my brother there alone when he's in danger!"

Giorgio's massive frame barrels back toward me. I squeak as he pins me to the mattress.

"*You* are in danger, Aurora. Have you ever stopped to wonder what your uncle would do to *you* if he found out you knew? If he wants his son to inherit everything, I doubt marrying you off would be his first choice."

I shake my head. He closes his fist around my throat, but I hiss and push against his chest.

"No one would ever accept me as the Achilles heir while Tristan is alive." He quirks an eyebrow as though I'm stupid. I whack his shoulder. "Then why are *you* the Vivaldi heir and not your older sister?"

"Because I *am* a Vivaldi." He's too loud. Too angry. Too close. "Tristan is not an Achilles. If anyone—"

"Don't shout at me!" I yell as panic washes over me.

There's light. His body is warm over mine, but he's much bigger than Tristan's newborn body. My aunt isn't screaming. I'm okay.

His mouth closes over mine, and I kiss him with every ounce of desperation trapped within my nightmares. When he pulls back, tears wet my face and misery squeezes my chest.

"This doesn't change our plans, Giorgio," I begin, despite the emotions clogging my throat. "I can't abandon my brother, and we can't kidnap him without starting a war, but I needed to tell you. I'm sorry I didn't tell you earlier. We can null the prenup. I don't want—"

"I don't care about the fucking prenup, Aurora. I care about you. I can rebuild wealth, but I can't replace you. I love you, *mia topolina*, you smart, stubborn, frustrating woman. I need you."

Too many emotions burst from me. As he pulls me into his lap with the comforter bundled around me, I respond to his declaration of love the way I wish I'd gotten to the first time.

"I love you, Giorgio. Please don't hate me. I need you, too."

"I could never hate you, Aurora."

"Promise?" It's shameless of me to ask, but I need his affirmation.

"Promise," he says.

I pull his lips down to mine and seal his promise with a kiss.

He's a man of his word, after all. It's sneaky and dirty to pull a promise from him without revealing my health issues, but I'm too strung out to handle more, and I'm desperate enough to use the dirty play.

I need and love Giorgio Vivaldi, and I'll do anything to protect and support him, even if it means risking my health and safety.

I now have two people to love and care for. Tristan and I aren't alone anymore.

We have Giorgio Vivaldi, the most ruthless, protective, and trustworthy mafia don in all of New York City.

CHAPTER 16

Giorgio Vivaldi

AURORA ACHILLES, MY BRIDE-TO-BE and cherished *topolina*, is the Achilles heir. This changes everything, no matter what she says.

Not between us. I believe her when she says she doesn't want either mafia empire. She's worked too hard for too many years to prove she doesn't want it. Hell, she's eighteen years old and already accomplished more than most men do in their entire lives, just so she and her brother could walk away from said empires.

Despite wanting to strip her of the blanket and shuck my pants off for a few hours of carnal fun, I carry her to the bathroom and stand her in the shower before stealing the quilt from her.

The pink-stained mess between her thighs sends perverse pleasure down my spine. Guilt rises, but when I unfasten my trousers, her green orbs sparkle with interest. I pull the material off my legs and stand naked before her for the first time. Masculine pride fills my soul as she swallows and studies me with hungry eyes.

She's too perfect.

I turn on the shower, adjust the temperature and pressure, and pull her to me. She wraps her arms around my waist and lays the side of her face on my chest. When she shifts and wriggles closer, I realize she's standing on her tiptoes to press her ear over my heart.

She's an enigma. My enigma. Sweet, sassy, smart, and stubborn.

I grab the back of her thighs and lift her off her feet. She wraps her legs around my waist. Lust hardens my cock. Her nipples pebble against my abs.

Ready to sink into her tight body again yet needing her able to walk later today, I sit on the bench, lean back against the wall, and brace my feet apart. She squeaks and lifts her face. I cup the back of her head and brush my lips side to side over hers before teasing her into deepening the kiss herself. She moans and wiggles her hips, trapping my cock between us, while hooking her hands together behind my neck.

When I pull her back by her hair, she whines and rubs her breasts over me. I snarl against her lips.

"I know you're sore, but I need you again, *mia topolina*, so I'll let you set the pace this time." I nip her swollen bottom lip. "Take what you need from me. Touch me. Hurt me for hurting you. My body is yours, so use it to ease the ache in your pussy."

Her breath stutters. She leans back, testing my restraint, and looks down our bodies with fascinated eyes. Her nose wrinkles.

"We're still gross."

"Then wash us."

Her pupils shrink. Expand. She nods her head and looks away just long enough to locate the soap, then meets my gaze.

Her silent demand has me on my feet before I tell my body to move. I grab the body soap, loofa, shampoo, and conditioner and drop them on the bench before sitting back down.

The wet glide of her body on mine pulls a groan from my chest.

I don't know how long she teases us both, but I'll never shower again without getting hard from remembering her hands on me as bubbles trail down her pert breasts. She tests my control with her innocent yet bold exploration of my body. I tell myself to take my hands off her and let her do as she wishes, but I need to touch her. Her sounds of pleasure and flushed cheeks as I grope her slim hips, narrow waist, thighs, and arms join my wet dream fodder. I find her hidden erogenous zones—avoiding her breasts and pussy—and enjoy her eager responses.

The hickeys on her throat and the dark purple bruise on her shoulder fill me with pride. I want her to carry my marks every day for the rest of her life.

Deciding the ones already on her body aren't enough—especially since I did them under duress—I give her more when she leans forward and licks the well of my collarbone. She moans and grinds her slick pussy along the underside of my shaft.

"Are we clean now?" I ask.

My throaty voice echoes in the steam.

She nibbles on my Adam's apple before responding.

"Not for long," she promises.

When my cock jerks, she smirks and wraps her fist around my tip. I hiss and clutch her hips. Diabolical delight brightens her emerald orbs. She begins my unraveling with slow, measured strokes of her fist as she grabs my wrist and brings my hand to her face. With awe-inspiring confidence, she nips, licks, and sucks each centimeter of my hand, taking each finger into her mouth and swirling her tongue over me.

I never knew my calloused, tarnished hands held so many nerves, but as she worships and adores them, pearly white fluid leaks from my tip. When she rises onto her knees and angles my cock between her legs, I groan her name and drop my head back.

She demands I watch and rubs her clit with my dick.

I'm powerless. I can't resist. She claims every ounce of my attention as she slowly, slowly works me into her body. About halfway down my shaft, her thighs tremble and uncertainty flashes in her eyes.

"Did you really fit before?"

I chuckle.

"Yes. You took every inch."

"No wonder I'm so sore. Maybe this is enough this time?"

Every muscle in my body bunches in rebellion, but I offered her control. I can't take it from her.

"Rub your clit, *mia topolina*. Lean forward and let me lick your breasts. We'll see what you think then."

When she follows my suggestion, I fall even more in love with her. She's truly too perfect.

I struggle to hold back my release as I fill my mouth with her breast and leave a few marks for my pleasure as she works herself up to a glorious orgasm. With every inch of me buried in her pussy, she squeezes me from root to base. I lose control, pull my wrist from her grip, grab her hips, and lift her halfway off my shaft.

Bracing my heels for better leverage, I surge up into her over and over again until her entire body contracts in a much stronger orgasm. Her flushed breasts and expression of euphoria tip me over the edge. I release deep inside her body in epic waves until my head spins and my bones feel hollow.

She slumps against me and wraps her arms around my nape. I stroke my digits up and down her spine until the sensitivity in my cock lessens enough to leave her tight, swollen sheath. Her quiet moan as I pull out echoes in my mind.

I give us both a quick clean before turning off the water and wrapping her in a towel. Her lopsided grin is too fucking cute, so I sneak a taste of her mouth and help her wrap her hair in a second towel before grabbing my own and securing it around my waist.

I lead her to the double sink and vanity and wrap my arms around her from behind. Our reflection steals my breath. She's so tiny compared to me.

"I didn't know what products you use, so I bought the best brands. Whatever you don't want, we can get rid of and go shopping for whatever you like."

"By *best*, do you mean most expensive? *Porca miseria*, Giorgio, this is… too much."

"Nothing is too much if it's for you."

She sighs and leans her head back against my chest.

"I'm tired," she murmurs.

I check the clock on the vanity and kiss her temple before guiding her to her sink.

"You can take a nap after you get ready."

"Ready for what?"

"We're going out. No questions. Just dry your hair and pick a comfortable outfit from the closet. I'll take care of everything."

When she nods and scans the counter with a slow blink, I elect to keep my hands off her for a while so she can recover, so I busy myself with getting dressed, but when she emerges from the closet in the flowy dress with shoulder cutouts, I can't resist. I kiss her exposed flesh and rub her arms as I guide her to the bed.

After a few halfhearted complaints, she lets me tuck her under the sheet and walk away before I give in to temptation and join her. The sight of her in my bed feels so right I almost slide in next to her, but if my headstrong woman insists on returning to her familial home—which she will, no matter what I say, then we can't spend the entire day wrapped up in each other like I crave.

I leave the bedroom door open and plod through the house on bare feet, enjoying the cool wood floors on my soles. After an extended moment of studying the counter and remembering the slow unveiling of Aurora's flesh, I tuck the memories into my spank bank and start a pot of coffee. Before my mind envisions all the ways I can savor *mia topolina* throughout the kitchen, I lean against the fridge and pull out my phone.

Several minutes later, with research completed and a plan solidified, I send Fiero a few texts before stalking out to the garage.

We left every door open between the kitchen and the vehicle—including the driver's door—and Aurora's lacy black panties hang off the edge of the seat. I pocket the scrap of material and give the inside of the car a quick wipe down before closing up and heading inside.

With a cup of coffee in each hand, I ascend the stairs and set one on the bedside table before retreating to the corner chair to watch her sleep.

Thirty minutes later, I wake Aurora and offer her the coffee. She shakes her head and pushes it away with an adorable scowl.

"I can't drink coffee or tea," she says.

My senses sharpen at her use of the word can't instead of don't, but her mussed hair and sleepy eyes steal my attention. She looks too kissable and soft in her disheveled and slightly confused state. I fight the urge to pin her to the bed and have my way with her.

Guilt clears my thoughts as she rubs her face with her hands in obvious exhaustion.

"How about some orange juice?" I ask.

She grimaces and rubs her temple before nodding and murmuring a polite, *"Yes, please."*

"Do you have a headache?"

She shrugs.

"I don't think so? Just tired and maybe a little dizzy."

I drop to my knees beside the bed and push her hair back so I can study her face. The pallor of her skin worries me.

"What can I get you?"

She blinks and trails her fingers over my face as though she needs to confirm I'm actually beside her.

"Orange juice sounds good," she whispers.

It's too much. I steal a quick kiss before forcing myself toward the door.

"Stay here. I'll be right back."

The sheets rustle. I turn as she swings her feet to the floor. As I open my mouth to admonish her, she pushes off the bed and stands, only to crumple like an accordion.

I dart across the room and catch her before she hits the floor. Terror and adrenaline flood my veins as I gather her limp frame into a cradle hold and sit on the bed.

She jerks awake and tries to sit up, but I snarl and tighten my arms around her.

"Be still, *mia topolina*, and let me hold you for a minute."

After getting her bearings, she sighs and leans against me. I study her for a few minutes as my panic slowly recedes.

She's not a scrawny preteen anymore, but having her flop around in my arms triggered memories of the day she passed out in front of me.

"I'm okay. I just stood up too fast."

"Does this happen often?"

"No, but can you blame me for needing a system reboot after what you did to me?"

The cheeky mirth shining from her eyes assures me she isn't on death's doorstep, but she's still too pale for my liking.

"I need to pee. Like, now," she insists.

I carry her into the bathroom and wait outside the water closet before scooping her up again.

"Really, I'm fine. I'll feel better after that juice you offered."

I hum a noncommittal response and take her to the kitchen. Her blush as I set her on the counter erases her pallor, and after she drinks a glass of orange juice, she seems back to normal.

But when I move her to the couch—refusing to let her feet touch the ground along the way—and make a quick trip to the bedroom for socks, she's half asleep when I return. She wakes and offers me a rueful smile as I strap a new pair of sandals onto her feet.

"How did you know my sizes?" she asks.

I kiss her ankle and trail my fingertips up her legs as I stand.

"Our mothers. Whatever they're scheming, at least it's thorough."

The front door opens and Fiero calls out, wisely making noise and announcing his presence long before stepping into the foyer.

I stop Aurora from standing and join her on the couch before responding to Fiero. He stalks in, takes the situation in with a glance, and sits in the armchair catty corner to us.

A profound sense of rightness settles over me as I introduce them.

"Aurora, this is Fiero Capito, my future consigliere. Fiero, meet Aurora Achilles, my fiancée."

As much as I love my sisters and Tristan, these are the two most important people in my life. I'll spend more time with them than anyone else in the world.

Fiero scowls as he leans forward and props his elbows on his knees.

"I told you, I'm not consigliere material."

Before I can correct him, Aurora beats me to it.

"And I'm not wife material, yet here I am. Grow some balls and accept the position already, would you? He won't take no for an answer, and you know it."

After a moment of stunned silence, Fiero smiles and sits back.

"I knew I was going to like you, boss lady. It's good to see someone besides me is on this mongrel's side."

I toss the car keys at him before he can piss me off any further.

"We can chat in the car. I already ordered takeout to eat as we drive, so let's go."

Fiero catches the fob and shakes his head as he stands.

"I'm not a chauffeur, either."

"You *weren't* a chauffeur," Aurora chuckles before gasping and clinging to me when I grab her and stand.

Fiero takes one glance at us and accepts his fate without another word, turning toward the garage. He leaves every door open behind him as he leads the way to the vehicle. After shutting the car door behind me, he goes back into the house to close everything down before dropping into the driver's seat and adjusting the controls. He's a big man, but my shoulders are broader, so he doesn't need to adjust much before backing out of the garage.

When he whips out into traffic, I consider admonishing him for trying to kill us, but Aurora's head settles on my arm. I take her hand and trace her delicate digits with mine.

Fiero pulls up to the restaurant and accepts our food. Aurora rouses at the smell and hums in delight as she digs in.

Despite the mirth shining in his eyes through the rearview mirror, Fiero doesn't make a suggestive comment about me working her too hard. When I pass him a burger, surprise flashes over his features, but he accepts.

After we all take a few bites, I nudge Aurora's shoulder. She looks up and smiles.

"This is so good. I didn't even realize I was hungry. Thank you."

I shamelessly lick a crumb from the corner of her mouth before righting myself and hooking my arm over her shoulders.

"Tell Fiero what you told me about your brother, *mia topolina*," I demand.

She chokes in surprise and downs half her water before scowling at my ploy.

Yes, I made sure she had delicious food—in a secure location with no prying eyes or ears—before throwing my demand at her.

Fiero's expression turns to stone as he processes the news. I appreciate his quick mind as he analyzes the situation before meeting my stare in the mirror.

"So what's the plan, boss?"

"Later. Right now, we're sharing info. You're next, consigliere. What's the latest with Nico Russo?"

"They tried to hack into your sister's tablet, but he got an anonymous tip and stopped it from happening."

I meet Aurora's wide eyes. She drops her hand to my thigh and furiously chews and swallows so she can answer my silent accusation.

"Yes, it was me. I sent the anonymous tip. I'm sorry I hid it from you, but I didn't really *know* you yet, and I just needed to protect your sister. I didn't mean to dig further, but—"

"What do you mean, *further?*"

I can't hide the anger in my tone.

She looks around the car as though she might find an escape before squaring her dainty shoulders and meeting my stare head on.

"I traced the malware back to the creator and sent every computer IP, phone number, and GPS location involved to Nico's assistant."

Fiero laughs.

"You didn't send it. You changed his desktop background. He logged on and nearly shit himself. She's a fucking genius, boss."

I harden my expression despite her mask of innocence.

"Since when did computer science equate to hacking?" I ask.

"Since… now?" she counteracts.

Fiero laughs harder, making me fear for our safety, but he avoids an overzealous cabbie and weaves through the traffic with ease.

"I swear, the two of you were made for each other. Boss, you better put a ring on her before she realizes she's too good for you."

I shift my hand into Aurora's hair and pull her to me for a kiss. She balks, murmuring something about burger breath, but I don't give a shit.

I'll do more than put a ring on her finger.

I'm marrying Aurora Achilles.

Today.

CHAPTER 17

Aurora Achilles

MY INSIDES THROB as Giorgio mercilessly kisses me. I thought, after this morning, I'd need time to recover before wanting sex again, but my future husband proves me wrong. So wrong.

Arousal hardens my clit and dampens my panties. The bruises on my neck, shoulders, and breasts throb with pleasurable pain.

He pulls away and tips my burger to my mouth, insisting I return to my meal.

"Do you need your computer from home to do what you do?" he asks.

I shrug.

"Not really. It'll take a few more minutes on start up to cover my tracks, but I can use any device you hand me."

"I have a job for you."

Surprise flares through me.

"Actually, *you* have a job for you, since everything is yours anyway."

"Wait, what? How is everything hers?" Fiero asks.

"We signed a prenup," Giorgio says.

I lean forward and meet Fiero's eyes in the rearview mirror.

"Tell him he's insane and needs to take it all back. I don't want it."

"Like he'd listen to me? Too bad, boss lady. Sounds like you're getting everything, even if you don't want it. Two everything's, actually. You know he won't let the Achilleses stiff you of your birthright."

"I don't want that, either! Give that to Tristan. I don't need it, and I never will."

"I'll worry about the Achilles family, *amore mio*. I'll keep Tristan safe. I'll secure his future.

Maybe I won't start a war as I do it, but no guarantees," Giorgio says.

If my burger weren't so tasty, I might throw it in his face, but before I get the chance to yell at him, he pulls me back in the seat, tucks me against his side, and tilts my chin up to meet his gaze.

"You will protect the Vivaldi and Russo families from cyberattacks. You'll find whoever is behind this, but you will *not* risk your safety, and you will *not* go rogue. We will discuss everything before deciding what's next. *Capisci?*"

I stare in amazement at the intensity shining from his dark chocolate eyes.

When I read the prenup, I thought he was crazy to trust me. I am not qualified to manage what he's built, but this?

This I can do. I *want* to do this. Already, my mind creates a list of tasks and adds resources I should compile before I even begin.

"*Mio Dio*, you're gorgeous. You've already started planning, haven't you?" Giorgio murmurs. He skims his fingers over my jawline and pulls me tighter against him. My seatbelt digs into my hip, but I don't care. The discomfort is worth it to be near him.

"I'm crashing the car if you start making out in the backseat," Fiero announces.

"My car. My wife," Giorgio snarls before kissing me.

I curl my toes in my sandals and wiggle in my seat, only to grimace when I smoosh my burger.

He pulls back and chuckles.

"Finish your food, *mia topolina*. We're nowhere near done for the day."

My heart thuds at the promise in his tone, but my stomach demands more, so I take his advice and chow down. When I decimate the burger and still have room for more, I reach for the bag, but he pulls it away and insists on feeding me fries two or three at a time.

Fiero parks the car and says, "I'll scope the place. Be back in a second."

Giorgio pulls a mint out of the bag and offers it to me.

"Do you have gum instead? Sugar doesn't agree with me," I say, mindful of all the warning signs my body has given me over the last three days.

He opens the center console and pulls out a pack of sugar free gum. I take the pack and thank him, but as an idea forms, I look between him and the gum a few times.

With embarrassment and arousal heating my face, I shove a piece in my mouth and chew a few times while I unwrap a second piece. When I pinch the end between my teeth and angle my face up to his, his chocolatey eyes turn liquid.

He leans down and kisses me so thoroughly I lose track of our surroundings, and when he pulls back, the gum I'd pre-chewed is no longer in my mouth.

I stare at his jaw as he enjoys both pieces of gum. Lust pools low in my abdomen as the tendons of his face flex.

Fiero raps on the window.

I shove a new piece of minty freshness into my mouth. Giorgio's pointed glance at my lips robs me of my thoughts. He plans to steal this piece, too.

When he wraps his long fingers around my thigh and demands I wait for him, my bra chafes my hard nipples and my damp panties cling to my sex.

I wait in a daze as he walks around the vehicle and opens my door for me, but when I realize we stand in front of a boutique dress shop, skepticism runs down my spine.

If it were a bridal store, I'd say hell no and stomp in the opposite direction, but the window displays a mix of colorful summer and fall outfits, so I don't balk.

Giorgio leads me inside and demands I try on at least five outfits before choosing my favorite. I walk around the store and choose exactly five dresses, because I'm sure as hell not trying on more.

My mother buys my clothes online and sends me to a tailor to ensure they fit. I don't care about fashion and never have, except for the one time she made me wear the ugliest, frilliest dress to a wedding.

The wedding where I passed out after pulling Tristan away from Giorgio.

After the attendant hangs my choices up in the dressing room, I thank her and slip inside.

Giorgio follows and snaps the curtain closed behind him.

"What are you doing? Get out," I half-whisper, half-hiss.

He backs me up against the mirror and leans down, but I turn my head at the last second and clamp my teeth together.

He won't fool me. I'm not done with my gum. He can't steal it yet. Plus, now that I'm on my own feet for the first time in what feels like millennia, I realize how sore and swollen I am from his claiming.

He pulls my hair and growls against my temple.

"I'm sore. Like, really sore," I admit.

With a frustrated groan, he presses his forehead to mine and strokes my hair back with both hands while reluctantly pulling his hips away from mine.

"You just want to torture me, don't you, *mia topolina*?"

I pull my lower lip into my mouth to hide its trembling and shrug. I want him. I really, really do.

But I don't think I'd survive another round of sex today without serious injury.

He yanks himself away with a curse and sits on the padded bench before spreading his knees and leaning back on the wall.

In jeans and a black t-shirt, with his arm and neck tattoos on display, he's incredibly dangerous to my health.

Maybe I don't need to walk ever again. He'd carry me around everywhere if he broke me, right?

I turn around and reach for the first dress before I cause my own ruin. Gluttony has never been an issue for me before, but I've also never been alone in a dressing room with Giorgio Vivaldi after losing my virginity to him before.

Careful to avoid my reflection and his eyes, I remove the dress I took from Giorgio's closet—which still had tags on it—and try on the first outfit.

It fits me well, but I didn't realize it had weird tassel thingies on the built-in belt, so I scrunch my nose and reach for the zipper to take it off, but Giorgio's masculine rumble stops me.

"Spin around first. Let me enjoy you," he says.

I take a steadying breath and humor him with a slow turn around.

"What don't you like about it?" he asks.

I pull the tassels away from my body and grimace. He chuckles and gestures for me to try the next one.

I catch his eyes in the mirror as I rise from taking off the *no, thanks*, dress. Lava swirls in my veins. My chest tightens.

I take the next dress off the hanger and put it on with an extra wiggle. He leans forward, braces his elbow on his knee, and bites the side of his thumb.

"What's wrong with this one?" he asks.

Right. Dress.

It's so comfortable and soft I forgot what I was doing. I look in the mirror and freeze.

"Nothing. It's perfect. I don't want to try on any others."

The simple cut accentuates my barely there curves while the jewel-toned fabric makes my emerald eyes pop.

"What will you do to get out of trying on the other three dresses?"

"What?"

"We're negotiating here, *amore mio*. You're talking about denying me three more strip teases. What will you do instead?"

My heart pounds against my sternum. He's serious. *Very* serious.

He leans back and crosses his arms over his chest. His jeans strain around his erection. I glance at the curtain.

"No one will rush in to save you, and no one will investigate what they hear, *mia topolina*. Everyone in the store knows what's happening in here. Choose, before I take what I want."

I move before I lose my nerve. Even though my first sexual encounter was giving him head, it's still frightening. He's so big and powerful, he could take control and suffocate me without even meaning to.

I drop to my knees in front of him and unbuckle his belt before meeting his eyes. My insides melt. Heat pulses between my legs. Saliva floods my mouth.

He gathers my hair in his fist and kisses me, scrambling my brains and stealing my gum.

I unzip his jeans, reach in, and pull out his massive cock. His thighs bunch as I explore his length.

I don't know if my efforts equate to three strip teases, but I enjoy every intense moment as I lick, suck, and stroke him until he loses control and releases in my mouth. After I swallow every drop, he pulls me into his lap and worships my mouth with his. When he pulls away, sets me on my feet, and tucks his cock back into his jeans, equal parts satisfaction and disappointment spear through me. I brought this massive, deadly man pleasure.

The only thing that could've made it better would be if I'd found my own release. But the heat pulsing through me is also addictive enough for me to forgive him.

It isn't until I check my reflection that I realize I'm chewing a massive wad of gum.

He tucks me under his arm and heads to the curtain.

"Wait, I need to change back into—"

"No. You're wearing this dress—the one *you* chose—for the rest of the day."

He flings open the curtain. The attendant gives a covert yet knowing look. Embarrassment steals my argument.

After paying and taking the bag containing my old dress, he leads me back to the car.

I like the dress even more the longer I wear it. The hem teases an inch or two above my knee, giving me enough fabric to feel flirty yet not worry about revealing too much.

Giorgio settles into his seat and pushes the hem higher to grab my thigh. Torn between oversensitivity and wanting his hand to wander, I bite my bottom lip and stare blankly out the window until he tucks me against his side.

I doze without meaning to, so when the vehicle stops, I jolt awake and check the clock, afraid he drove around in circles again to give me time to sleep, but less than five minutes have passed. My head throbs and the world spins.

Maybe sex isn't for me. I mean, I love it and want more of it with Giorgio, but what if my body sees it as stress instead of pleasure?

Sadness roars through me. A life without sex seems way too pathetic. I can understand why some people become addicted. When Giorgio kisses my knuckles, I sigh and tell myself to stop being so morose.

He opens his door and warns me not to get out on my own. I nod and study the area.

A mix of townhouses and businesses line the street, like hundreds of others in New York City, but nothing looks familiar. Parallel parked along the side of the road with cars of all makes and models, Giorgio's vehicle blends in a little too well. I turn to look out my window at the building we're parked beside and realize the nondescript shop could sell anything. Anything.

Apprehension jangles up my spine, but as Giorgio opens my door, my anxiety fades away.

He won't let anything happen to me. No danger will make it past him. His eyes never stop scanning the area for threats, and his muscles remain poised for action.

I take his hand and plaster myself against his side, refusing to be a distraction when he clearly isn't comfortable on the sidewalk.

He opens the foggy glass door and ushers me into the building.

Fiero stands in the back corner beside a tall woman dressed in all black. I stiffen until her white gloves and polite smile register.

She welcomes us, bids us closer, and gestures to the table draped in black cloth beside her. Eight jewelry display cases sit side by side.

I swallow as emotions clog my throat. Each display case holds a set of male and female wedding rings.

I never expected to have any say over what my ring looked like, even though I'd wear it the rest of my life. My mother made it clear long ago she'd be in charge of every aspect of my wedding, including this, so I don't know how to process all the emotions welling up in me.

As we move closer, I realize two matching necklace and bracelet sets—one feminine and one masculine—sit in their own displays behind the rings. I glance at Giorgio. His diabolical smirk almost releases the floodgates, but I breathe in through my nose and shake my head.

"What is this, exactly? Why are we sneaking around for wedding rings when our parents want everyone to know we're together?"

Giorgio pulls me flush against him, wrapping me in his arms and easing me further from my outburst.

"These aren't normal rings. Each piece of jewelry has its own micro-GPS tracking device. They connect through both satellite and cellular systems, so no matter where you go on the globe," he leans down to press his forehead to mine, "I'll find you."

My breath hitches. I hook both hands behind his nape and offer him my most innocent expression.

"Are you sure about this? You won't be able to fake your death and run away from all your problems if I put one of these on your finger."

"Oh, I'm sure, *mia topolina*. You're stuck with me for the rest of your life."

I clear my throat and blink a few times.

"Thank you, Giorgio."

"Don't thank me yet. Try them all on. If none of them suit you, I'll buy you a new one tomorrow. And the next day. And the next, until the only jewelry you own are things I've bought you."

Touched beyond measure, I frame his face with my hands and kiss his cheeks, nose, chin, and forehead before pulling away to look at the rings.

I dismiss the first three. They're too big and gaudy, but the fourth and fifth have simpler arrangements, so I stop and study them for a moment. The sixth steals my attention. It's elegant, but the diamond sticks out too far from the band. I don't want to gouge chunks out of Tristan when we play fight.

The craftsmanship on each one is superb. I don't know where they've hidden the micro-GPS chips; they all look like normal jewelry to me.

Emotion surges through me when I step in front of the seventh ring.

"What is this one called? I've never seen a diamond cut like this."

"It's a kite cut, also known as a delta cut. All our diamonds are natural and certified to ensure the highest quality, but this one has flawless clarity and is the largest colorless diamond to have gone through the certification process this year," the saleswoman says.

My brain turns off as she continues praising the set. All I know is that it's beautiful and I want to see it on my finger. Tiny diamonds sparkle in the simple vine designs framing the center diamond. The matching necklace and bracelet hold a similar delicate design.

The thicker, more masculine ring has vine designs etched along the surface and a matching kite-cut diamond embedded in the band.

Giorgio reaches over and slips the feminine engagement ring and wedding band from the display. My entire body shakes as he takes my hand and slips them on my finger. After kissing my knuckles, he tilts my wrist and shows it to me.

"I love it," I manage through tingling lips.

He smiles, turns me around, tucks my hair over my shoulder, and puts the necklace on me. I shift toward the full-length mirror and can't recall ever feeling so beautiful.

He wraps his arms around me from behind and closes the bracelet around my wrist. I blink back tears, annoyed when they blur my vision, and lean back into his chest, but he twirls me around and drops to one knee.

Confusion spears through me. I'm already wearing the ring, and we're already betrothed, so he doesn't need to propose.

He pulls a large jewelry box from behind his back—which was *not* there when we got out of the car—and holds it up toward me.

"What are you—?"

"Hush, *mia topolina*. It's my turn to ask the questions."

I stand frozen in shock as Giorgio Vivaldi, the most terrifying, ruthless, and honorable mafia don in NYC, opens the case and proposes.

"Aurora Achilles, will you marry me?"

I can't breathe. Tears escape my lashes and emotions clog my throat.

Nestled inside the large jewelry box is a complete set of GPS jewelry and accessories—watch, necklace, ring, shoelace tags, and sunglasses—cool enough to make any eight-year-old boy envious.

My heart threatens to burst. By offering me this, he's including Tristan in our future. I don't have to worry about losing my brother anymore.

"Yes. Yes, I will marry you, Giorgio," I sob.

Fiero lifts the jewelry case from the table and brings it to me, even though Giorgio's ring is the only thing left in it. I pull it out with shaking fingers and turn to Giorgio.

He towers over me.

"How about right now?" he asks.

"What?" I half-sob, half-laugh.

He's not making sense.

The front door opens and Mrs. Tamsin walks in.

Giorgio's lawyer. Marry him right now?

After a moment of pure, instinctual panic, logic and love cut through the mayhem and dry my tears.

"Yes. Right now. Where do I sign?"

Giorgio's arms surround me. His tongue invades my mouth. I close my fist around his ring and kiss him with all the joy in my heart. When he lifts his head, the wonder in his gaze matches the awe pulsing through me. I grab his massive, tatted hand and slip the ring on his finger before peppering his knuckles with kisses and wrapping my arms back around him.

I'm not alone anymore.

I love Giorgio Vivaldi and he loves me.

He'll protect my brother. I'll protect his sisters. We'll secure a safe, happy future for everyone we love.

Together.

CHAPTER 18

Giorgio Vivaldi

EVERY TIME SHE LIFTS her hand up in front of her to study the rings sparkling on her finger, a smile pulls at my lips. I can't help it. She's stunning.

I lean back, pushing my knees into the back of the passenger seat even though it's pushed as far forward as possible, and slip my hand under her hair to play with her nape.

The large black jewelry box sits open on her lap.

"Will Tristan wear those?" I ask as I tease the flesh around her necklace clasp.

She shivers and smiles at me.

"He's always asking for a slimmer watch, so he'll love this one. I just wish he could video call me from it like he can his current one."

I wrap my hand around her nape.

"You didn't hear a thing the sales lady said today, did you?" I ask.

Her sheepish expression is too much. I swoop down and take the kiss I've been dying to share with her ever since our last one ended.

When I lift my mouth from hers, my half-hard cock throbs in my jeans and her cheeks redden in a blush.

"He can video call, voice call, and text from this watch," I say against her mouth.

She pulls back and lifts the box in disbelief.

"What? How? There's no way there's a camera, speakers, and microphone hidden in this tiny thing."

I chuckle and point them out to her, but she remains skeptical.

"My watch can do the same, but your bracelet doesn't have a screen or camera, so you're limited to voice calls."

"Show me," she demands.

We connect Tristan's watch to her phone and play around until she's convinced. I smirk and lift her hand to my lips.

"Every piece of jewelry has an emergency button. You press it, I find you."

"Button? On my ring? Where?"

When I point them out to her, she shakes her head in amazement.

"I can't believe I've never heard of these before. I mean, I know you can buy GPS jewelry online, but this is another level. *No one* would suspect these are anything but pretty. How did you find them?"

"He didn't find them. He special ordered them," Fiero interrupts.

I send him a glare.

"When? We learned we were getting engaged less than four days ago."

"I placed the order when I couldn't take you home with me that first night," I snarl.

"All eight sets?" she squeaks.

"I meant what I said earlier, Aurora. If you didn't like any of them, I'd keep trying until I got it right."

"You're crazy," she whispers.

As I cup her face and worship her lips, Fiero's mumbled, "You can say that again," filters through my ears and prevents me from taking the kiss too far.

I lift my face from hers when Fiero rolls to a stop at the gate to the Achilles' familial estate, but Aurora chases me with a whine. I wrap my fingers around her throat and nip her bottom lip.

"You can wear your engagement ring, but not the wedding band," I mutter against her cheek.

She huffs and holds her fist against her chest, almost as though she's daring me to take it from her, before sighing and offering me her fingers. I slip the delicate band off her dainty digit before tucking it into a ring case and wedging it into my pocket.

"No one takes it off but me, *capisci*?"

She nods and fiddles with her engagement ring before meeting my eyes. The yearning in her emerald orbs solidifies my plans for the evening.

She just became fully mine. My lover. My wife. My future. I'm sure as hell *not* letting her leave my sight for the next lifetime.

We can't leave Tristan to her family, but tonight will be the last night she returns home. If it means war between the Vivaldi and Achilles families, I don't give a shit. As long as Aurora, Tristan, and my sisters are safe, everyone else can eat a bullet.

Or taste my knife.

Fiero parks the car and quirks a brow at me through the rearview mirror.

"Stay in the car and on the premises. We'll be back in a few minutes," I say.

Aurora grabs my hand before I step out of the vehicle.

"Wait, why would *we* be back? I'm not—"

With the door halfway open and one foot on the ground, I lean back toward her and steal a quick kiss. When I pull back and she gives my lips a dreamy look, I chuckle and exit the car. By the time I reach her door, an angry blush colors her cheeks and she glares at me, but when I offer her my hand, she takes it without hesitation.

As I lead her up the stairs, she dons her emotionless mask, and even though I hate losing sight of her honest expressions, I nod my approval. When I interlock our fingers and give her a gentle squeeze, reminding her this is no longer her home, she offers me one last vulnerable smile before battening down the hatches for battle.

Her mother welcomes us at the door. After a polite greeting, she gives Aurora's new outfit a critical once-over before escorting us to the sitting room. She launches right into updating us on her preparations for our announcement party next week until I pull Aurora's hand into my lap. My wife's ring glitters against the dark blue of my jeans, and even without the wedding band, it's stunning.

Madona stiffens and stops talking, but despite the fury and curiosity in her gaze, she doesn't ask.

I thank her for taking such great care of us and ask to borrow both of her children for the evening.

She agrees, but she doesn't have much choice, does she?

"Is that why you're in such casual attire? You want to take Tristan out to dinner?"

"Yes. He'll miss our announcement since he'll be at camp next week, so I thought an outing was appropriate," I say.

She nods and requests he be back by his curfew, as though she's a normal mother instead of a cold bitch who locks her children away every night. When the side door opens and Tristan greets the cook, Madona's entire countenance sours.

I wonder when she last saw her son beyond locking his door. Does she peek into his room before she jams the key into the lock, or does she secure him away from the world without sparing him a glance?

I may have had a fucked up childhood, but no matter how horrible life was, at least I knew I had a mom who had my back even if I was wrong, solely because we were family.

Aurora's reassuring smile as Tristan peeks into the room soothes the ache in my heart.

Madona calls him in, but after formal greetings, he stands near his sister. For half a second, pure joy shows on his face when his mother announces our dinner plans, but he tucks his enthusiasm away and thanks us all with annoying propriety.

I navigate us out of the conversation and house before we run into any other household members.

Tristan glares at me when I wrap my arm around Aurora's waist, but when I nudge her elbow, encouraging her to hold his hand, he forgives me and asks where we're going.

I counter by asking for his top three favorite places to eat, then lob those options to Aurora to make the final decision. When she laughs, all traces of consternation leave Tristan's face.

I open the rear passenger door and tell Tristan to scoot all the way to the other side so Aurora can sit between us. He approves of the arrangement and nearly launches himself across the seat.

When I introduce him to Fiero, both man and boy size each other up for a moment before

Fiero reaches over his shoulder and offers Tristan his hand. After they shake, Tristan lobs an impressive volley of questions at the battle-hardened mafia man, who answers each one without missing a beat, somehow maintaining his normal dry humor while keeping it child appropriate.

Aurora claims Tristan's attention and gives him my gift. His excitement wriggles deep into my chest. He hooks his watch up to his phone and dons every item except the sunglasses. Even the shoelace trackers go on his sneakers before we reach the restaurant.

We end up eating dinner in a little mom-and-pop diner a few streets away from Tristan's school. When I usher Aurora to sit in the corner and take the chair beside her, Fiero tucks Tristan into the chair across from her and boxes him in by taking the outer chair.

We must look ridiculous—two tatted, muscular men scowling at anyone who dares glance at the stunning woman and young boy sitting with us—but we can't let our guards down when so much is at stake.

Tristan becomes more animated as he scarfs down pizza, breadsticks, salad, and pasta. Aurora relaxes and enjoys his antics while picking at her food, but when she seeks my hand under the table, I decide to not press her to eat more. The tears shimmering in her animated emerald eyes stem from joy and wonder, so I ask for a to-go box and save her pizza for later.

With how tiny she is, I always expect her to eat small portions of low-calorie foods, but she surprises me every time with her appetite. I've never seen a specialty pizza with steak strips, extra black olives, extra spinach, a slew of other veggies, and very little cheese, but she seemed to enjoy every bite she took. Even though she didn't eat as much as I would like, she still finished an entire slice.

As I lead us back to the car, Fiero covers our backs, keeping Aurora and Tristan between us, where they're safest. Tristan's full belly catches up with him once he's tucked in the car. He slumps against Aurora's shoulder a few minutes into the drive. We enjoy a comfortable silence the rest of the way, letting tomorrow's worries wait until tomorrow as we digest both the food and the intimacy we found around the dinner table.

Fiero stops the car in front of the Achilles family home.

I steal a quick kiss from Aurora before slipping out of the car and walking around to Tristan's side. When I open his door and rouse him, he mumbles and rubs his eyes, but settles back onto Aurora's shoulder.

I scoop him up and wait for *mia topolina* to scoot closer before offering her my hand. Her hungry eyes wander over my forearms as I help her from the vehicle. If I flex a little more to make my veins a bit more prominent, it's because Tristan is precious cargo—and I like the appreciation in Aurora's gaze.

I send Fiero away for the night. He doesn't ask questions, even though he probably expected to drive me back to the townhouse tonight.

I carry Tristan into the Achilles mini castle and settle him into his bed without interruption from other household members. As Aurora slips into the bathroom to warm a washcloth, I pull off his shoes and slip off his necklace. After wiping his face and arms, she gives him a kiss on the forehead and plugs in his phone before pushing me toward the hallway.

I turn off the light. She closes the door. I scoop her into a cradle hold and carry her into her room.

Her whispered argument fades as I kiss her. I push the door closed with my heel and let her feet slip toward the floor.

Piece by piece, I remove our clothes, leaving them strewn throughout the room, and slide us both under the sheets. She whimpers and writhes underneath me as I take my time exploring her with my mouth and hands. Heat builds between the sheets, but I keep *mia topolina* tucked underneath, unwilling to expose her in case her mother walks in.

In no rush, I play with her nipples and lick every inch of her chest. Her legs tighten around my waist. I crawl backward and worship her flat stomach and tease along her hipbones before continuing lower.

I press my palm over her mouth just in time to muffle her cries as I run the flat of my tongue over her sex. Unable to resist, I nibble and tease even as she fights and begs me to stop, until her honey coats my face and her pleading devolves into wordless whimpers and moans. I ease my tongue and tease along either side of her clithood, careful to avoid direct stimulation, and slowly press two fingers into her tight, swollen pussy. When she bites my hand, magma escapes from my balls and sears the inside of my shaft, so I surge up her body and plaster my mouth over hers. With two digits sunk deep inside her, I thrust my hips and run the underside of my cock over her clit.

She comes in long, epic convulsions as I growl into her mouth and stroke her G-spot with my fingers. As she soaks my hand, the sheets, and my cock, I lose control and fill her bellybutton with my release. I shudder and dive deeper into her mouth before gentling my kiss and slipping my fingers out of her body. My pearly white seed overflows her bellybutton and seeps down her sides.

I yank a few tissues from the box on the bedside table and use them to soak up the worst of our mess before tossing them in the trash bin and pulling her close. She shivers and wraps her arms around my waist.

"Just for a few minutes, *capisci*?" she mumbles, already half asleep.

I hum a noncommittal note and pull her leg over my hip before fixing the blankets and tightening my arms around her.

Her breathing changes into the steady cadence of sleep and she snuggles closer.

A little more than half an hour later, the door handle rattles. Aurora's mother swings open the door, but she stops it halfway, no doubt shocked at the clothes strewn all over the room. Less than a second later, she closes the door.

I smirk into Aurora's hair as her mother rushes down the hall toward the stairs without locking the door.

With *mia topolina* tucked safely against me, I fall into a deep, dreamless sleep. Time skews. At one point, screaming echoes in my head, but Aurora's quiet whimper overrides all else, so I pull her on top of me and rumble nonsense until she settles.

Despite being in the viper's den, I wake in slow increments. Aurora's scent surrounds me. Soft sheets brush against my naked body. A keyboard clicks quietly nearby.

Aurora no longer lies in the bed with me.

I surge awake and find her in front of her computer. With the screen illuminating her mussed hair and my black shirt dwarfing her slim frame, she's effortlessly sexy. The clock reads early morning. Tristan's alarm should go off any second.

The sheets beside me are cold.

"How long have you been up?" I ask.

Aurora jumps and whirls around with her hand over her heart.

"Holy shit, you scared me," she gasps.

Insult rolls over me.

"Did *mia topolina* forget she had a dark and dangerous mafia man in her bed?"

She shakes her head. A tiny smirk tugs at her lips, but her thoughts tug it into a frown.

"No, but I think I found—"

She stops talking when her mother's door opens and footfalls head our way. I lift the covers.

Aurora turns off her computer screen and dives into the bed with me.

Her mother passes our room and unlocks Tristan's door as his alarm sounds. Aurora tucks her face against my chest and hooks her digits over my shoulder. I skim my fingers over the back of her thigh and tease behind her knee.

She's too tempting. I trace over her hip and fill my hand with her naked ass. Her breath hitches as I grind her damp pussy against me.

Water rushes through pipes in the wall as Tristan gets in the shower.

"Wait, let me shut down the computer. It's not safe," Aurora whispers.

Her breath ghosts over my sternum, but I let her go and will my cock to soften as she slips out from under the cover.

When she bends over the keyboard, the hem of my shirt lifts and teases the lower swell of her ass.

I rise from the bed and grab her hips. She hisses and tries to push me away, but I growl and reach under my shirt to fondle her breast.

"Don't mind me, *mia topolina*. Focus on the computer. I'll focus on you."

Mindful of our surroundings, I use my fingers to bring her to a quick orgasm and spurt my release onto her back. In a moment of insanity, I scoop the viscous fluid up and sink my coated digits into her fluttering pussy. She looks over her shoulder at me with wide, vulnerable eyes.

"You're too fucking sexy, *mia topolina*," I murmur.

She blushes and shifts her weight.

"Are you done on the computer?" I ask.

She nods.

I kiss the exposed flesh of her shoulder from my too-big shirt's neckline before pulling my fingers out of her pussy and helping her strip.

Tristan turns off his shower. I point her toward the bathroom and pat her ass before gathering all my clothes. After a quick soap and rinse, I towel dry and dress in yesterday's clothes.

The clothes I wore when I married Aurora.

She emerges from the closet and rushes through the rest of her morning routine. I steal a kiss before leading her into the hall.

After a simple breakfast, we send Tristan off with Mr. Hearthright and head back to Aurora's room for her purse.

My phone vibrates in my pocket. I answer my sister's call and stop mid-stride when her distraught voice sounds through the speakers.

"Mamma called Camilla, Giorgio. I don't know what she said, but Camilla's gone non-responsive. Her nurses called me because they're concerned," Serenity says.

Aurora walks out from the bathroom with her brows drawn in worry.

"I'm going to visit Camilla now, but I'd like to know what mamma said before I get there. Can you go talk to papà?"

I meet Aurora's eyes. She hesitates, but nods and grabs her bag from beside the desk.

"Yes, I'll head over right now. Is Nico going with you?"

"Of course."

After saying a rushed goodbye, I hang up and send Fiero a text. He replies with a *yes, boss*.

Madona intercepts us before we escape out the front door. I apologize for the impromptu sleepover—playing it off as an accident—but she insists I am welcome any time.

I thank her and lead Aurora outside. The overcast sky and foggy morning air increase the dread forming in the pit of my stomach.

After settling Aurora in the seat behind Fiero, I grab my travel hygiene bag and my clothes bag from the trunk before dropping into the back passenger seat.

Fiero drives down the lane without a word. Aurora opens her mouth to speak, but stares in fascination when I pull my shirt off over my head. She strokes my ego with her dazed appreciation as I strip out of my jeans and maneuver my body in the limited space of the car. When I lift my hips and pull on my trousers, she sucks her bottom lip into her mouth and presses her knees together.

My naughty girl enjoys a good strip tease.

With my pants unfastened and my half-hard cock straining in my boxer briefs, I lean back and grab her nape. She hisses and glances toward the front seat before I tug her closer.

Fiero clears his throat.

I'll murder the *stronzo* if he so much as mutters a single word. After a tense meeting of eyes in the rearview mirror, he decides he enjoys his life enough to not end it early and keeps his mouth shut.

I grit my teeth and tuck in my shirts before adjusting my cock and fastening my trousers.

Aurora turns toward her window with her bottom lip trapped between her teeth again. I lean down and tie my dress shoes.

She sends me furtive glances as I rise, thread my arms into my suit coat, and shrug it into place. When I fish my cufflinks from my bag and move to secure them like normal, her dainty hand settles on my wrist. I'm powerless to deny her when she offers to help. With trembling fingers, she fixes my cuffs and slips each cufflink into place before leaning over me and pulling my tie from my bag.

I cover her hands with mine and meet her eyes. Her gaze softens. She smiles.

I lean forward to give her better access to my nape. She flips my collar and circles my neck with the tie.

She's the only one I'd allow so close to my throat, and going by her expression, she knows it. She knots and tightens my tie with sensual grace before fixing my collar and smoothing her hands down my front. I lean over and take her mouth with all the emotions welling up in me.

The car slows. I pull back as Fiero coasts through the gates to my familial home. Aurora's expression flips through several emotions before she dons a bland mask.

As she stares at the house I grew up in, I recall how startled she was this morning when I found her at the computer instead of in bed beside me.

She uncovered something, but her mother interrupted us before she could tell me, and the morning has been so busy, I forgot to follow up.

Despite the early hour, the front door opens and my mother steps out to greet us.

My vision narrows as frustration and fury coalesce within me.

I never realized how cold and calculating my mother was until she led the conversation of my betrothal, but now, with her standing in full makeup and elegantly dressed with a serene, welcoming smile as dark clouds drift across the morning sky, all I see is the villain in Camilla's story.

She may not have swung her fists at my older sister, but she sure as hell isn't supporting her. I fully agree with Serenity's assumption: whatever my mother said to Camilla sent her into a mental spiral.

I need to know what she said so Serenity can help Camilla.

I can't let my parents fail my siblings anymore. *I* can't fail them anymore.

Aurora takes my hand and gives it a gentle squeeze, offering me her support and reminding me of what's at stake.

I should leave her in the car, but I need her by my side.

I open the car door and pull her out after me before tucking her against my side and starting up the stairs.

No matter what happens, I'll never be a clueless bystander in my own family again.

It's all because of Aurora.

Aurora Vivaldi.

My wife.

CHAPTER 19

Aurora Vivaldi

GUILT WRIGGLES IN MY GUTS, but I push it aside and focus on the task at hand. With the fury wafting off Giorgio, maybe it's a good thing I couldn't tell him what I found this morning. There's no doubt he'd burn too many bridges if he knew I suspected his uncle paid someone for the cyberattacks.

In fact, I think Narciso Vivaldi is behind the physical attacks on his sisters, too, but I don't have concrete evidence yet, so it may be best to focus on helping Serenity and Camilla instead of muddling his thoughts with suspicion over his uncle.

Bianca Vivaldi offers us an overly bright and innocent greeting, but Giorgio wants none of it.

"What did you say to Camilla, Mamma?"

She quirks a brow and rolls her shoulders into an even haughtier stance.

"Only what your father and I agreed on."

"Which was?"

Giorgio's gritted response raises the hairs on my nape.

Maybe I should retreat to the car, but his arm over my shoulders prevents me from slipping away.

He wants me here. I can't leave. I *won't* leave.

"*Mio figlio*, we only want what's best for Camilla. Come in and have some breakfast, then you can discuss this with your father."

I settle my hand on the small of his back as he grinds his teeth.

"We'd love some breakfast," I lie.

Looks like we'll have to play a little good cop, bad cop to figure out what she said to Giorgio's older sister.

I haven't seen Camilla in almost ten years, but both Serenity and Giorgio will do anything for her, so I will, too.

Giorgio would do the same for Tristan. I can't *not* reciprocate when I love this jerk so much.

We follow his mother to the table. He pulls out my chair and settles in the one beside me, placing himself across from her while the head of the table lies empty for his father.

Another full place setting waits across from me.

My head spins without warning.

Giorgio takes my hand under the table and sandwiches it between his thick thigh and huge palm. I squeeze his leg and drink half a glass of water, willing my nerves to settle. His eyes narrow on my face.

Bianca launches into a spiel about our upcoming announcement party and the schedule for wedding preparations. I find it difficult to smile and nod, but she doesn't need to know it's all pointless. Giorgio and I are as much a husband and wife duo as she and Matteo are, but we must continue our ruse until we find a safe escape route for Tristan and corner the culprit behind the attacks on his family.

The minutes drag by until Matteo Vivaldi finally arrives.

His brother follows close on his heels. A shiver runs down my spine as Narciso Vivaldi's eyes trail over me, but I flex my fingers into Giorgio's thigh and offer the older man a polite smile.

He settles in the seat across from me. The servers fill the table with tray after tray of food. My unease grows. Giorgio's frustration becomes more apparent as his parents show a despicable lack of concern for his sister.

Mio Dio, I'm tired. I should have stayed in his arms all night, but my curiosity pulled me to my computer.

My mother didn't bother us this morning. Or last night.

I pause as I realize I skipped two doses. It shouldn't affect me too badly, but life has not been easy lately, so I excuse myself and swing my purse over my shoulder.

I don't stop Giorgio from coming with me, but I ask him to wait in the hall for a few minutes. He glances between my purse and my face a few times before nodding and kissing me.

"Be quick, *mia topolina*, or we'll have a repeat of the last time I followed you into this bathroom. *Capisci?*"

Heat thrums low in my belly. I nod. He opens the door, flicks on the light, and pushes me inside.

I place my purse on the counter, pull out the pill pouches I keep tucked in the bottom, and empty one onto my palm. After chucking the pills into my mouth, I turn on the faucet, stick my face in the sink, and swallow the vitamins. Needing a few more sips to clear my mouth of the aftertaste, I hear nothing but rushing water until I turn off the faucet.

Raised masculine voices filter in under the door from the hallway. I zip my purse closed and tuck it over my shoulder before opening the door. Giorgio's broad back blocks me from seeing his father, but Matteo's words ring clear in my ears as I turn off the light and step out of the bathroom.

"Camilla is my daughter, so if I tell her to do something, she'd better fucking do it. Same goes for you, *mio figlio*. I don't care how boring or simple the Achilles girl is, you'll marry her without a fuss because I told you to."

Giorgio steps toward his father, and even with his back to me, the menace wafting off him sends ice down my spine. I reach for him.

A hand closes around my upper arm and yanks me backward. I fall against Narcisco's wiry body with a surprised squeak.

Giorgio pulls me away from his uncle and shoves me into the bathroom.

"Don't come out, no matter what you hear. I'll open the door when it's safe."

The solid wood door slams shut. Pitch-black darkness envelopes me. Sounds of violence sneak under the door.

My mind splinters. Ice infects my entire body. I hug my purse to my chest and stumble backward until the wall catches me.

Matteo's shouting morphs to my aunt's screams.

I sink to my butt in the darkness with Tristan's tiny newborn body in my arms. We can't make a sound. They'll kill us.

I can't breathe.

My aunt's screaming fades to eerie silence. The doorknob turns.

I failed. They heard me. We're both dead.

Tristan won't survive because of me.

Light blinds me. My eyes won't focus. A masculine voice echoes from far away.

I can't break the ice shielding me from the world. I'd rather stay frozen forever than face the horrors of reality.

Arms wrap around me and lift me from the ground. Warmth seeps into my side. My head throbs.

A deep, rumbling voice sneaks into my bones and begins my thaw. Fragrant heat wraps around me, the smell familiar and comforting. As the ice melts from my flesh, my limbs tingle and burn as though frostbitten, and my surroundings come to me in disjointed, jagged pieces.

"You're okay, Aurora. I've got you. You're safe. Tristan is safe."

I know that voice. I trust that voice.

Giorgio Vivaldi.

My husband.

He's here. He's holding me. I'm okay. I'm safe. Tristan is safe.

Pain spears up my arms and my fingers ache. My chest heaves as though I ran a marathon. Sounds buzz in my ears.

I blink until Giorgio's handsome face comes into focus. He strokes my hair and continues murmuring assurances as I slog myself into the present.

"*Mio Dio*, I'm sorry, Aurora. I'm so fucking sorry. I didn't think beyond getting you away from my uncle, but I should have realized how similar that bathroom was to a closet."

I blink a few more times before his words make sense.

He closed the door. It was dark and violent. I was alone with my brother.

No. Tristan wasn't with me.

I look down and find myself wrapped in Giorgio's suit coat. His cologne and the warmth of his body still emanate from it, and I want nothing more than to stay wrapped up in it forever, but my brain insists I check on my baby brother—even though logic demands he isn't here—so I wriggle and panic when something small shifts against my chest.

"Be still, *mia topolina*. You're okay."

My jaw refuses to unlock, so I can't explain, and my brain won't form words anyway, so I fight harder.

He growls and pulls open his coat.

Crimson trails down my arms as I gouge my flesh with my nails, but relief spears through me when I see my purse, not my newborn brother.

Tears scorch my face and sobs wrench from my chest, pulling words from the nightmares lingering in my mind.

"She's dead, Giorgio. I heard them kill her. I heard everything. I sat in the pantry with Tristan *right here*—" I pound my chest and sob, "—and listened to them murder her. She told me she'd open the door when it was safe, but she never did because she was *dead*. Gone forever. They killed her."

Soothing hands stroke me from head to toe as I break away from reality, unable to process the emotions pouring through me. I cry so hard I puke and shake so badly my bones ache. As I fall to pieces, Giorgio holds and supports me, giving me a safe place to purge eight years' worth of trauma.

When nothing but a hollow shell of memories remains, I slump against my husband's broad chest in exhaustion, knowing he'll protect me while I'm at my weakest.

"Just breathe for a few minutes, *mia topolina*. I have you. You're safe."

I close my eyes and listen to his heartbeat. The hush of the soundproofed vehicle as it weaves through the city sinks into my awareness and becomes the first part of the world beyond Giorgio's protective cocoon.

He presses a water bottle to my lips. I drink. Cool liquid soothes my raw throat.

"Better now?" he asks.

I shrug and meet his concerned gaze.

"Tell me more, Aurora. Who died?"

"*Mia tia*, Chiara. Otello's wife. The only good thing about that man. She was the mother I had never had. I was in the kitchen warming Tristan's bottle. He'd just come home from the hospital. So tiny. Only five days old. I had *no* idea what I was doing. *Mia zia* rushed in and pushed us into the pantry."

Even as I hear myself speaking in disjointed sentences, I can't force my brain to smooth out my story. I just need to tell it.

"I did it right that time. The bottle. Tristan didn't fight or cry. He drank the whole thing and went to sleep without a sound. I think he knew. He still knows. He has nightmares."

"Do you have nightmares?"

I shake my head. Blink. Nod. My lips tremble.

"Yes. My parents argue. They scream a lot. I can't sleep. I hear *mia zia* instead. The men laughed at her while she screamed. They mocked her as she died, and all I did was sit there in silence."

Warm, calloused hands frame my face and force me to focus on Giorgio's dark eyes.

"You did the right thing, Aurora. You protected yourself and Tristan. It's what your aunt wanted."

"No! I should have—"

"You were only ten years old when Tristan was born. How many men did you hear? Two? Five? Ten?"

I shake my head, not sure of the answer.

"It doesn't matter, *amore mio*. One man is too many. You were a ten-year-old girl. Hiding was your only option."

If my head weren't so hollow, I'd cry more tears. He brushes his thumbs over my cheeks.

"You survived, Aurora. That's all that matters."

I nod. Maybe I believe him, maybe I don't. I can't tell with the fog filling my brain.

"We're done for now. You can't handle more, so just relax in my arms for a few minutes. We're almost home."

I nod again and slip into an exhausted half sleep. When the world shifts and I hear a masculine voice coming from a chest other than the one I press my ear against, I jolt awake. I relax as I recognize Fiero's frame. He opens the doors to the townhouse in front of Giorgio as he carries me inside.

I curl my fingers into my husband's shirt, needing his warmth more than my next breath. He toes off his shoes mid-stride and settles us on our bed with his back against the headboard. After requesting a few things of Fiero, he gathers all the pillows close, almost building a fort around us, and extracts my purse from my grip before pulling the blankets around me. It's too stifling.

"You're shivering. Stop fighting."

"I'm not cold."

"Maybe not, but let me care for you. Be still."

All my strength seeps from me. I'm too tired to argue, so I relax and enjoy the firmness of his arms.

Fiero returns with a tray of snacks and three steaming mugs. Giorgio trails his thumb over my brow.

"I asked him to sit with us for a debrief. He'll leave in a few minutes, but this can't wait."

Fear sparks through my nerve endings.

"Did you kill him? Your uncle?" I ask.

"No, but I should have," he growls.

"Giorgio! You can't—"

My words jumble in my mind as he snarls and grabs my chin.

"He touched you, Aurora. He put his filthy hands on my wife. I don't care if he's blood. He's a dead man walking."

The promise of death in his eyes warms my heart.

It doesn't make sense. I abhor violence. His threat shouldn't pebble my nipples or make my clit throb, but my body responds as though he whispered filthy words in my ear and nipped all my sensitive bits.

I grab his collar and give us both a vicious shake.

"No! You can't kill him, not yet. Not until I find solid evidence."

Giorgio stills. Fiero freezes with his hands still on the tray, half-bent over the bedside table.

"Evidence of what?" Giorgio demands.

He pries my fingers off his collar and gathers my wrists into one of his hands, never taking his eyes off mine. I swallow.

"I think he hired whoever's behind the cyberattacks. Possibly coordinated Camilla's car crash and Serenity's kidnapping, too."

He tightens his grip around my wrist before setting my hands in my lap and spearing his fingers through my hair.

"My father went to great lengths to keep those incidents under wraps. How much digging did you do last night?"

I shrug.

"Obviously not enough if I don't have evidence," I grumble.

"Then what do you have? What pulled you out of my bed last night and made me wake to empty sheets?"

Shock spears through me at the depth of emotion in his voice.

I swallow before answering.

"I know you have enough shares in all your father's companies to overtake him without force. I know he's clueless you're the one buying all his collateral and assets because you use different subsidiaries and smaller businesses to cover your tracks. I know you've suspected it was an inside job for a while but couldn't pinpoint who it was."

Fiero stands and shakes his head as he drops into the nearest chair. Giorgio presses his fingertips against my scalp, demanding my attention.

"You found all that in one night?"

"It's not like you're trying that hard to hide what you're doing, so it was easy to find. And I wasn't doubting you; I was profiling you. I scanned for abnormalities along the way, just like I did for Nico Russo and your father."

A muscle ticks in Giorgio's jaw.

"Why do you suspect my uncle?"

"He's skimming off your father, but he's not sending the money to the typical offshore accounts. He's paying someone and has been for a while, but they've been smart and keep changing modes of contact and location and… everything. I just need a little more time, and I'll have what you need to prove to your father it's your uncle," I say.

"You're hoping for a peaceful takeover, aren't you, *mia topolina*?"

I nod. He scowls and tightens his grip on my head.

"It no longer matters if my father knew or not. Neither man is fit to be the head of my family anymore. They've both earned the humiliation and pain I've prepared for them."

"He's your father, though. He's Serenity's father. He—"

"Sat by and did nothing while she was kidnapped. He hasn't lifted a goddamn finger since—"

Both Giorgio's and Fiero's phones buzz in their pockets. It must be a vibration pattern set for emergencies, because they stiffen and look at each other.

At Giorgio's nod, Fiero stands and heads out the door as he pulls his phone from his pocket.

"What is it?" I ask.

Disappointment flattens my willpower as Giorgio lifts me off his lap and settles me in the middle of the mountains of pillows.

"This isn't something you should be a part of, *mia topolina*. I'll leave my computer password on the desk and my car in the garage, but I should be back before it's time to pick up Tristan. Stay here and rest. *Capisci*?"

I nod and fight a sense of abandonment as he stands. His eyes soften and he leans down for a quick, reassuring kiss before disappearing.

I wait until the front door closes and the security system engages before rolling onto my side and pushing half the pillows onto the floor. The steam swirling up from the mugs on the bedside table catches my attention. As I rise onto my elbow, the smell of apples and cinnamon warms my heart.

Giorgio remembers the smallest details.

Maybe he already suspects I'm not as healthy as I pretend to be.

Fear tightens my gut even as cotton fills my head.

He wants a child. Why else would he have pushed his seed inside me this morning? Even if he proclaims to want me more than his money or power, he's shown many times that he yearns for a baby of his own, and he's never once balked at our parents' demand for an heir. Will he still love me when he finds out I can't give him what he wants most?

Too wrung out to handle more worry, I prop myself up on the headboard and sip the apple cider.

When I feel more like death warmed over instead of a frozen corpse, I set down the mug and swing my feet toward the floor. A mini pep talk to myself and a few steadying breaths later, I slowly stand and shuffle to the bathroom. After cleaning the dried blood off my arms and scrubbing underneath my nails, I head to Giorgio's study.

I may as well have been hit by a semitruck with how stiff and sore I am. Every muscle in my body aches, every joint creaks, and every tendon strains from overuse.

Panic attacks suck.

I use the password Giorgio left, grateful for his trust, and focus on what's most important: proving Narciso Vivaldi stabbed Matteo Vivaldi in the back and put the entire family in danger.

A little more than an hour later, my phone chimes from the bedroom. I push myself to my feet and wobble up the stairs to fish it out of my purse.

Mr. Hearthright's voice fills the line the second I answer.

"I'm so sorry, Ms. Achilles, I need to bring Tristan home early. My family—"

My heart rate spikes and adrenaline floods my veins as his voice breaks. I toss my bag over my shoulder and slip my feet into my shoes as I answer.

"How soon will you drop him off?"

"We're pulling into the drive now. I wouldn't do this if it weren't an emergency."

"I know, Mr. Hearthright. It's okay. Tell him to go straight to his room. I'll be home in five minutes."

"Of course, Ms. Achilles. I'm terribly sorry."

I end the call and rush down the stairs to the garage. The seat, steering wheel, and pedals take an agonizingly long time to adjust, so by the time I open the garage door and shift into reverse, urgency pulses behind my sternum.

I've only driven a handful of times beyond earning my license, but I match the aggression of the city drivers around me and make it home faster than I thought possible. I park near the front door and send Giorgio a text as I rush into the house. With every step I take, dread builds in my chest, so when my mother doesn't greet me at the door, I sprint up the stairs.

I swing open Tristan's bedroom door and breathe a sigh of relief when he looks up from his phone. He cocks his head. I plop down on the bed beside him.

"You okay? Did mamma see you come home?" I ask.

He shrugs.

"I haven't seen anyone since I got back. No one. Not even the chef. Man, it sucks about Mr. Hearthright's family. I wanted to go to the internet café and see my friends," he whines.

I check the time on my phone. My text to Giorgio remains unread.

"I'll take you. Let's go," I say.

Even as Tristan hoots with excitement, my unease grows. I tuck my phone back into my purse and stand as he gathers the things he scattered all over the floor and shoves them back into his bag.

"Actually, I was in too much of a rush to get back to ask. What happened to Mr. Hearthright's family?" I ask.

"He got a call from the hospital because they were in a car accident. I think they were all badly hurt. He looked scared."

I wait until he zips his bag and stands before I give him a hug.

"That must've been scary for you, too," I say.

After a quick squeeze, he pushes me away and shrugs.

"I gotta pee, then I'm ready," he declares.

"Okay, I'll wait for you in the hall. Which café were you going to? I'll put it in my GPS."

"Are you driving?"

His skepticism doesn't bother me. The streets of New York City are terrifying.

"Well, we're not taking a cab or the subway, and asking a driver means we have to get permission from mamma, but I have a car, so…"

I dangle the fob from my finger.

He smiles and bounces on the balls of his feet.

"Then let's go!"

When he heads for the door instead of the bathroom, I chuckle and step in front of him.

"Go pee first, you numbskull. Which café?" I ask.

He yells the name as he hurries toward the bathroom. I open my map app and step out into the hall.

Arms wrap around me from behind. My phone clatters to the floor and skids under the decorative table near my mother's door. I open my mouth to scream, but a masculine hand covers the bottom half of my face, blocking my nose and mouth.

Otello Tempe's cloying cologne clogs my sinuses.

I jab my heel backward into his shin. He hisses and lifts me off my feet. With my arms plastered to my sides and his hand over my mouth, I can't break free or warn Tristan.

"Hush, Aurora. Open your bedroom door for me. I'll be quick. Unless you'd like your brother to join us?"

I shake my head. My lungs burn.

"Open the door," he snarls into my ear.

His breath sends waves of disgust down my spine, but I twist the handle on my bedroom door. He pushes us inside and flings me onto the bed before turning and pulling a key out of his pocket.

A key. To my room. He has a key to my room.

Panic pounds through me, but I shove it away and gulp down oxygen as I scramble to my feet.

I cannot let him lock that door.

"Lie back down, little whore, or I'll rescind my offer of being quick," he snarls.

His hand lowers the key toward the lock.

I throw my purse at the back of his head before grabbing the nearest book off my shelf.

My ring catches the light.

I press the hidden emergency button and throw the book. Otello's curses ring in my ears.

He locks the door and turns toward me. Blood trickles down his nape.

I throw a second book. My vision wavers and head spins, but I grab two more books—one in each hand—and throw as I turn back toward him.

He blocks the first book, but the second bounces off his upper chest and nicks his throat. I scramble backward and grab more as he stalks toward me. He pulls a pistol from inside his suit coat.

My stomach sours as he lets it hang at his side.

"Put the books down, Aurora. I like your spunk, but don't take it too far."

When I don't move, he shifts his thumb and pulls the hammer back with a metallic click. The books slip from my fingers and thump onto the floor. He steps within reach. I cringe as he lifts his empty hand and cups my chin.

Tristan calls my name from the hallway. Otello smirks.

"Tell him your stomach hurts, but you'll be ready in a few minutes."

Bile rises in my throat as he brushes his thumb over my lips. His features twist in anger when I don't respond fast enough.

"I don't care if he's my son; his holes still work the same as every other little boy's. Tell him you'll be out in a few minutes, or I'll lock him in here with us and fuck you both."

I stammer out what I hope is an acceptable excuse.

Tristan pauses before asking through the door, "Are you sure you're okay? You don't sound good."

"I'll be fine, Tristan. Just go back to your room until I come get you."

After another stressful moment of silence, Tristan says okay and heads down the hall. His door opens and closes.

My insides curdle as the man I've always hated and feared smiles and spears his hand into my hair.

"Good girl. Now try to be quiet so he doesn't interrupt us again, yeah?"

He moves his body closer to mine. I instinctively lift my hands to push him away, but he presses the pistol's muzzle to my temple and chuckles. My bracelet slides down my wrist. I find the button with my thumb and mash it.

What if the jewelry doesn't work? What if Giorgio never comes?

Impossible. Giorgio promised. He always keeps his word. Always.

I use the conviction running through my veins to bolster my mind.

"I'd tell you to get on your knees, but your mouth doesn't interest me. It's the other holes I want. Did it hurt when Giorgio Vivaldi took your virginity? Has he had your ass yet?"

Tears gather on my lashes. I shake my head. Interest sparks in his eyes.

"Strip down and get on the bed. All fours. Ass up," he demands.

"Why are you doing this?" I manage through the lump in my throat.

He grinds his hips against mine. Vomit climbs up my throat at the feel of his hard cock against my stomach.

"Because I want to. I have all the power I need to do whatever the fuck I want, and what I want is to fuck you," his sneer seems more demonic than human, "so get on the goddamn bed before I decide to get rid of you like I did my whore of a wife."

All the blood drains from my head.

He just admitted to killing my aunt, which means he hired the thugs who broke into our house and murdered her while I hid in the closet. It was him. He's worse than I ever imagined.

When he pulls the gun away from my head and steps back, no relief spears through me. The room becomes suffocating. I need out.

He tilts his head in amusement.

"Strip, little whore, and let me see what I've waited almost two decades to enjoy."

My entire body goes numb. I can't do this.

Giorgio will save me. He'll bust down the door any second now.

Otello has a gun. I need to get it away from him somehow. Giorgio can't get hurt because of me, not when there are so many other threats closing in on him.

My heart cries out to the man who gave me everything—his wealth, his power, his future— because I need him.

I no longer dream of leaving the mafia. All I want is Giorgio Vivaldi.

My husband. My lover. My heart.

I need him. Now and forever.

CHAPTER 20

Giorgio Vivaldi

THE TIRES SQUEAL as I stop on the lawn of the Achilles family home. Smoke billows out around the bent hood of my vehicle, but I don't give a fuck.

They didn't open the gate fast enough and I need to be inside the looming mansion. Now.

Big red numbers blink on my watch's screen. Aurora pressed the emergency beacon almost four minutes ago.

Too long.

I don't care how far away I was or how much destruction I wrought to get here; four minutes is an eternity during an emergency, and my wife needs me.

A smaller set of numbers blinks underneath the first. Less than a minute after Aurora hit her alarm, Tristan engaged the emergency beacon on his watch.

As I bolt up the steps to the front door, three other vehicles screech to a halt in the grass. I don't wait for Fiero or the rest of my crew to join me before I slam through the front doors and stalk across the foyer.

Tristan looks up while rushing down the stairs. When he sees me, he turns and heads back up, yelling over his shoulder as I vault up after him.

"Rora's door is locked, but mamma isn't home, and she sounded weird when I told her I was ready to go."

"When's the last time you talked to her?" I ask as I pass him.

"Before I pressed the button. Something's not right. The house is never this empty," he calls up the stairs at me.

I reach the landing and run down the hall to Aurora's room. Her door handle cuts into my palm but doesn't budge, no matter how hard I yank on it.

"Aurora? Open the door," I demand.

She takes too long to respond, and when she does, the strain in her voice raises my hackles.

I pull my pistol from my belt holster, step back, drop my weight, and pour every ounce of power into kicking the door, driving the sole of my shoe into the wood near the handle.

Wood cracks and metal snaps, but the frame remains intact. I kick again and rush through the doorway, catch the door bouncing back with my shoulder, and snap my muzzle toward the masculine form on the far side of the bed.

Otello Tempe tugs Aurora between us, shielding himself with her body. He wraps his fist around her throat and yanks her back against him as he lifts his pistol and aims at my chest.

She grabs his wrist and rises onto her tiptoes when he squeezes her throat.

Fury tinges my vision red as I take in her lack of clothes.

Her bra hangs off her shoulders with the front clasp undone. Only her panties remain on her body.

Otello Tempe is a dead man walking. He'll never leave this room. I'll kill him.

He knows it, too, but he's too much of a weasel to die quietly. The moment his eyes harden with the knowledge of his imminent death, I step forward, ready to take a bullet at point blank range just so I can wrap my hands around his throat and squeeze the life out of him.

He presses his muzzle to Aurora's temple.

I freeze.

"Drop the gun and tell the men in the hall to stand down," Otello demands.

I move my finger off the trigger, extending it along the smooth metal, and lift both hands in the universal sign of surrender.

"Fiero, you heard him," I call over my shoulder. I slowly squat and place my pistol on the floor.

"Drop your other weapons while you're down there," the old man sneers.

I meet Aurora's shiny emerald eyes and pull a second pistol from my chest holster. She shifts her grip on his arm and leans away from him. He hisses and pulls her closer.

"Be careful, Otello, before I decide to make your death as slow and painful as possible," I say as I set the pistol beside the first.

He chuckles and digs his fingertips into Aurora's jugular. Her face turns purple before he relents, but she doesn't gasp or fight for breath. Instead, she holds eye contact with me.

"Keep going, Giorgio. I wasn't born yesterday. I know you have more weapons. Where are those infamous knives?"

His goading won't work. I pull the third pistol from my chest harness and place it beside the others on the floor.

"Really, though, is she worth all this fuss?" he mocks as I take the first knife from my chest harness.

Aurora grimaces as he presses the muzzle harder against her temple. I clench my fist around the hilt of my knife, struggling to remain in control.

She lifts her finger, indicating Otello's forearm, but I scowl and give a slight shake of my head.

She's watched too many movies. I'm not throwing a knife anywhere near her, especially not with her face so close to the target.

He grinds his cock against her back and speaks with his mouth next to her ear.

"Unless he doesn't know? You haven't told him yet, have you, darling?"

The disgust and sense of violation filling her expression ensures Otello will not have a quick and painless death. When his words register, her pupils shrink.

"She's just another piece of ass, Giorgio. She can't give you that heir you're so desperate to have."

I methodically place the knife next to the pistols and pull the last blade from my chest harness.

"There's no point to any of this if she can't pop out a few brats for you, is there? You should just forget all this and go find yourself a worthy wife," Otello continues.

I lift a brow and pause with my fingers still on the hilt of my longest knife.

"Then what would we do with Aurora?" I ask.

The *stronzo* smirks and releases her throat to trail his fingertips over her collarbone. His muzzle shifts away from her temple.

"Don't worry. I'll take care of her," he murmurs into her hair.

She slams the back of her head into his face and drops her weight. He grabs her hair and pulls the trigger as I throw my knife and lunge forward.

Otello screams. Blood sprays. I swing. As he stumbles backward from the force of my blow, I grab his wrist and punch the hilt of my knife, burying it deep into his arm so over an inch protrudes from the other side. His pistol clatters to the floor as I sever tendons and muscles, ruining his use of his hand.

Aurora twists, trying to free her hair from his grasp. I yank my knife from his arm and bury it in his shoulder. He screams and reaches for the hilt. I push Aurora out of harm's way and swing.

My knuckles crack against his cheek and fresh blood spurts from his nose and mouth. I follow through and thrust a left hook from the hips, connecting with his ear so hard shockwaves travel throughout my body.

He drops. I follow him down, straddling his prone form and unleashing my fury on his face, raining blow after blow on his increasingly uglier mug, until Aurora's shouting breaks through my mania.

"Giorgio, stop! You'll kill him," she pleads.

Less than a foot away, she stands with one hand on the back of her head and the other hovering between us, almost as though she can't bring herself to touch me.

I stand and shake out my arms, flinging blood onto the floor, and meet her gaze.

"That's kind of the point, *mia topolina*," I snarl.

She shakes her head and winces.

I run my fingers over her scalp, needing to assure myself she's okay. She hisses when I find the lump on the back of her head from where she headbutted her uncle. The size concerns me, but maybe it just seems bigger than normal because she's so small?

"Where else are you hurt?" I demand.

"I'm fine," she lies.

With splatters of blood on her bare flesh and her hair tangled from another man's hand, I need to mark her as mine and assure myself she's okay.

I cup the base of her skull, avoiding the contusion while holding her in place for my inspection. She shivers and clings to my lapels as I run my hand over her shoulder, hip, and back.

When I pull away, silent tears trail down her face, and her entire body shakes as her adrenaline drops.

Shouting echoes down the hall.

I shrug out of my coat and drape it over her shoulders. She threads her arms into the sleeves and overlaps the front. She's so tiny the fabric covers her from collarbone to mid thigh.

I guide her away from her uncle as he coughs and gurgles his way back into consciousness.

Fiero steps into the doorway, but before I can pass Aurora over to him, the telltale click of a hammer cocking sounds behind me.

I push Aurora forward, blocking her with my bulk, and hiss when fire streaks into my side. Fiero and I pull her down to the ground and cover her with our bodies as bullets pepper the wall. My consigliere passes me his favorite hand piece before pulling a second pistol from his belt.

With a nod toward Aurora, I tell him to get her the fuck out of danger. He lifts his chin in acceptance and grabs her arm.

The emptied gun clatters to the floor.

I surge upward and stalk around the bed. Otello lifts a loaded pistol from my discard pile and pulls the trigger a millisecond before my bullet pierces his brain. White-hot agony slices through my hip, but I continue forward and send bullet after bullet into his head and chest until his disfigured body lies in a pool of dark red crimson.

I kick his foot. He doesn't move. Blood oozes from his wounds. I tuck Fiero's pistol into my waistband and turn toward the door. My heart freezes in my chest.

Aurora's arm slips from Fiero's grip as they both fall to the ground. She lands on her knees and looks down at herself. When she opens my coat for a better look, red pours down her side.

Fiero's curses stream in the background as I lunge across the room and grab Aurora. I push my coat and her unlatched bra out of the way and inspect her wound.

"The bullet bounced off your ribs; it didn't puncture your lungs. You're okay, *mia topolina*."

"Damn straight it ain't in her ribs. The fucking thing is in my back," Fiero hisses.

I yell down the hall for my men and realize Tristan's voice has echoed from the bottom of the stairs since before Fiero appeared in the doorway.

Aurora grabs my forearms and lists to the side. I murmur a string of words, half-comforting, half-stern, as I guide her onto her back.

"I've got you," I say as I yank my long-sleeve shirt over my head and ball it up to press against her side.

She pushes me away.

"You're bleeding, too."

She's right. Fire streaks through my side and hip.

"It's nothing. I've had worse. *Mio Dio*, why are you bleeding so much? Stop fighting me. Let me apply pressure," I snarl.

She shakes her head and pushes me away again.

"Desk. Top drawer," she says.

Her words make no sense. Panic threatens to strip away my ability to reason as her blood soaks my suit coat at an alarming rate. I grab her wrists and move them out of the way before pressing my shirt to her side.

As she hisses, two of my men reach us. One kneels to assess Fiero while the second squats on Aurora's other side.

Tristan skids into view.

"Go back downstairs, Tristan."

Despite the warning in my tone, he ignores me. His eyes go wide as he sees the blood soaking Aurora's side. He jumps over Fiero in the doorway and weaves around me.

I can't spare a hand to stop him.

Aurora relaxes, and although she shakes from pain and shock, her eyes shine with relief.

Tristan drops beside me and tears open a sterile medical pouch. He reaches for my wrist, but after glimpsing the label, I lift my hand and the shirt away from her wound before he touches me.

She grits her teeth as he pours the entire packet of white powder into the gash. He jerks my hand back into place.

"Press hard," he demands.

Aurora closes her eyes and digs her nails into the back of my fingers. I shift my hand, keeping her wrists pinned to the floor, but offering her a better grip. I press my shirt against her wound.

Fiero passes his phone to the soldier helping him and tells him to speed dial the guy labeled *doc*. The man starts the call and puts it on speaker.

"It's not stopping! She's bleeding too much," Tristan panics.

Aurora shakes her head.

"Another. On my back."

Fuck, she's going into shock. She's too pale. Too lethargic.

She hasn't lost *that* much blood, but there's no denying her condition.

I roll her onto her side and, with the help of my soldier, pull her arm out of both my suit sleeve and her bra strap, and curse at the long, shallow laceration across her shoulder blades. I pass the rib compression over to my man and cup her shoulder to hold her in place as Tristan tears open another pouch.

"You'll be okay, *mia topolina*." I don't know if I'm reassuring her or myself, but I need to say something as Tristan pours the powder into her wound. "We'll patch you up and get you to my doctor—"

"She needs the hospital. Papa's physician couldn't help her at home, so she *always* had to go to the hospital," Tristan demands as he whips his shirt over his head and presses it to her back.

She groans and passes out for a few seconds before shivering awake.

"What's her condition called?" the doctor asks through the speaker.

Aurora's sluggish answer lodges a rock in my chest.

"Congenital sideroblastic anemia."

After a slight pause, my personal physician answers in his calm, no nonsense manner.

"Bring her to my clinic. I'll have a blood transfusion ready. Keep pressure on her wounds, even if you think the bleeding has slowed."

I curse and growl a confirmation before leaning forward and hooking her arm around my nape, preparing to roll her into my arms and stand.

"I'm sorry, Aurora. This is going to hurt," I apologize.

She shakes her head.

"No, get someone else. You're bleeding. Don't carry me."

"I'm not letting anyone else put their hands on you, and I need you in my arms where I can assure myself you're okay, so be still and let me take care of you," I snarl.

At my nod, my soldier helps roll her side against my chest, maintaining pressure on her wound as I wrap my arm around her back—over her laceration—and curl her tight to me. When I squeeze too hard, she wheezes and digs her nails into my nape, so I loosen just enough for her ribs to expand over a comfortable breath. I thread my other arm under her knees and rise.

"Get me a blanket or something to cover her with," I snarl.

I know she's injured, but I don't like knowing other men's eyes roam over her naked body. She's mine.

"No. Cold is good. Slows bleeding," she murmurs.

I demand my soldier drape the blanket over her anyway.

"Hey, boss, toss me one of them packets. I'll stay behind and oversee clean up," Fiero says.

When I nod, Tristan balks.

"But you're shot!"

"It missed all the vital things, so I'll be fine for a few more minutes. Go get the boss lady fixed up, and I'll be there before you know it, ready for a little pinch and pull."

I question my choice in consigliere. Slice and dice for a killing spree? Pinch and pull for bullet removal? This *pazzo* needs a lingo update.

"Thanks, consigliere." The soldiers look between us in shock as I call him my second for the first time, but I continue as though it's old news. "I expect to see you at the clinic in less than thirty minutes," I snarl.

"Yes, boss," he answers as he pushes himself up off the floor.

Tristan stands with several more packets of coagulant in his hands, glancing between me and Fiero, obviously torn on where to go.

"Come with us, Tristan. I might need you if she passes out again," I say.

He nods and hands the pouches to the nearest man before rushing to my side.

To the tune of Fiero delegating tasks to the men, I start down the stairs and shorten my stride so Tristan doesn't hurt himself trying to keep up, somewhat reassured when Aurora remains alert enough to dig her nails into my nape. I settle into the back seat of whichever car is ready to go, careful to keep pressure on Aurora's wounds, and let my soldier shut the door. As he and Tristan rush around the car to their seats, she turns her face into the crook of my neck and shudders.

"You're okay, Aurora. We'll get you patched up in no time," I murmur.

She nods and passes out. Tristan pats her shoulder and keeps her awake with random trivia, offering me a deeper glimpse into their lives before our unexpected betrothal. Favorite colors, shapes, sounds, time of year, and TV series episodes. Specifics surrounding key moments in their shared experiences. Jokes. Everything highlights how much they love and rely on each other.

I want to experience this intimacy every day for the rest of my life. I want to be someone who these two amazingly resilient souls can trust and love for the rest of their days. Neither one will ever hurt like this again.

The moment the driver parks outside the clinic, three nurses and my personal physician emerge. Tristan jumps out and runs around to open my door, but a male nurse reaches me first and leans in to take Aurora from me.

"Get your hands off. I'll carry her in," I snarl and stand, forcing him to move out of the way.

Tristan stays right on my heels as I rush into the building. When my physician leads us straight to a room, I follow him inside and stop beside the bed.

"Sit. Keep pressure on her wounds," Dr. Karl demands.

As I turn, he gestures for a nurse to lower the bed and grabs Aurora's wrist. He straightens her arm and cleans the crook of her elbow before starting her transfusion with practiced ease. With a few curt words, he sets his team into coordinated chaos. In less than two minutes, they've hooked Aurora up to several machines and monitors, coaxed her to take a few pills, gathered a ton of supplies, asked a few pertinent questions, stationed a nurse on either side of me, and prepped my physician for what looks like surgery.

He wheels his stool so close his knees brush against mine before he leans into Aurora's view. She gives him a slow blink. Although still sluggish and pale, she seems more alert than in the car.

"Have you ever been injured like this before?" he asks.

She croaks out a *no*.

"We'll wait a few more minutes for the oral coagulants to work and for your vitals to stabilize before I check your wounds."

She nods.

Dr. Karl leans to the side and lifts a brow.

"Mr. Vivaldi, you're bleeding all over my bed. Stand and I'll bandage you while we wait."

When I hesitate, Aurora digs her nails into my nape and traps my gaze within hers. The worry shining from her emerald orbs matches the fear thundering through my veins, so I stand and allow my physician to treat the wounds on my side and hip.

Tristan shuffles forward and takes Aurora's hand as my physician takes the nurse's spot at my side. Aurora blinks at him and attempts to give him a small, reassuring smile, but she passes out halfway through the motion. I tighten my arms around her, and Tristan squeezes her hand as she lies limp between us.

"She'll be okay, Tristan," I say, willing it to be true.

He nods and lifts worried eyes up to mine, but when he meets my hard gaze, he squares his shoulders and returns my nod.

"Yeah. We'll protect her together, just like we promised."

Emotions clog my throat, but I affirm our pact by saying, "Yes. Together."

She wakes and gives an unsteady sigh before closing her eyes and squeezing both my nape and Tristan's hand.

"I'm okay. Really. I already feel a little better," she mutters.

With clinical movements, my doctor tugs down my waistband and studies the oozing wound on my hip. His unimpressed expression reveals his thoughts. By the incessant throbbing and fire streaking through my hip, not only is the laceration deep in the muscle, but the surrounding flesh must be burned, too. The gash on my side bleeds freely.

He cleans and bandages me in record time before checking the monitor and studying Aurora's face.

Tristan squeezes her hand again before relinquishing his spot to my physician.

Two nurses help situate Aurora's IV lines as I lie her face down on the bed. She clings to my nape, but I duck out from under her arm, encompass her chilly hand in mine, and squat so my eyes are level with hers. I stroke my thumb over her knuckles, wishing I could gather her into my arms.

Dr. Karl and his nurses set to work again, cleaning, inspecting, and treating her wounds with seamless teamwork. She grits her teeth and closes her eyes until I nip the back of her hand and murmur her name. Even though the machines show her improving vitals, terror gnaws at my insides at the thought of her closing her eyes and never opening them again. She lifts her lashes and focuses on my face for a moment, but pain creases her brow and steals her attention.

Dr. Karl announces her bleeding has slowed but says pressure bandages for an hour or two would be best. She gives the tiniest nod before biting back a groan as they lift her off the mattress and wrap a bandage around her ribs and over her shoulders to compress both wounds. When they roll her onto her side and prop her up with pillows, sweat glistens on her pale brow.

A nurse pulls a chair up behind me, so I scoot it closer and sit at Aurora's bedside. Her hand still feels cold within mine, so I request a blanket and tuck our joined hands underneath when they settle a warmed sheet over her.

"I'll be back in an hour to check her bleeding, but the nurses will keep a close eye on her. The best thing for her right now is to rest, so we'll turn down the lights and bring in a cot for her brother." He gestures for the male nurse to fetch the mentioned cot before ensuring he has my attention. "Once the transfusion is complete, you can join her on the bed, but for now, it's safer to let her sleep solo."

I hate the logic, but I'd do anything to see her recovered, so I grind my teeth and nod my understanding. She belongs in my arms where I can feel her breathing and smell her scent, but with the IV lines, monitor hook ups, and her bandages, it would be too easy to hurt her instead of comfort her, so I rub my thumb over her wrist and prop my other elbow on my thigh.

As they settle Tristan along the wall on Aurora's other side, my phone buzzes in my pocket. I check the screen before answering Fiero's call. The male nurse offers me a pair of scrubs, which reminds me I'm shirtless and wearing bloody pants. Another nurse offers Tristan a clean pair of clothes, too. I put the call on speaker, set it on the edge of the bed, and thank the man with a nod as I take the clean clothes from him.

"We found Madona Achilles bound and beaten in her closet. Otello obviously r—"

"You're on speaker," I snap.

Two pairs of wide eyes stare at me. The anguish in Aurora's glazed gaze hurts my heart.

"I sent her to the hospital with half a dozen of our men for protection," Fiero says. His strained voice relays his pain. "The rest of the house is empty. Every single one of the staff is gone. Not even a guard at the gate."

Which explains why I had to smash it with my car.

"Where's Horatio Achilles?" I ask.

"I sent two men to confirm his whereabouts, but rumors say he's at his office. We'll make sure he hears about this from your perspective," Fiero replies.

"Thanks, consigliere. Anything else?"

"Cleanup is almost complete, so I'm heading your way. How's the boss lady? The men are asking about her," he says.

My stomach churns as I realize his hidden message. She left too much blood behind.

"She's stable and resting," I answer.

"Thanks, I'll relay that. See you in a few."

Just before I end the call, his hiss of pain and string of expletives fill the air as he curses the backseat of whichever car he's trying to lower himself into. I sigh and toss the clothes down onto my chair and move my phone to the nearby tray, refusing to release Aurora's hand for even a second.

"What's going to happen now?" Tristan asks.

Aurora lifts her hand to him. He steps forward and carefully takes it.

"You're going to come live with me. Both of you," I say.

Tristan swings saucer-sized eyes my way. Aurora's fingers stiffen within mine.

"Really? I can come live with you?" The excitement on Tristan's face fills my heart with warmth.

Tears swim in Aurora's eyes, but she relaxes and nods her head.

"Yes, Tristan. We can't stay with our parents anymore. It isn't safe."

By the worry lines on her brow, she's aware enough to realize the war she's tried so hard to avoid has already begun. The moment Otello Tempe put his hands on her was the moment Horatio Achilles lost everything.

I will show him no mercy.

A nurse clears her throat near the door. I turn to find her waiting with her finger hovering over the light switch. Her not-so-subtle reminder of Dr. Karl's order for Aurora to rest proves I've chosen the right medical practitioner. He's ensured his staff remain focused on the patient's needs.

"I'll go change in the bathroom," Tristan says.

"We have a shower in the on-call suite. I can take you there if you want a quick one," the nurse says.

Tristan shakes his head, but Aurora encourages him to go. He reluctantly follows the nurse into the hall.

The moment the woman closes the door behind them, Aurora's breath hitches. I lean down and cup her face, but she digs her nails into my hand and closes her eyes.

"You should change before he comes back," she whispers through a throat thick with tears. I kiss her brow and caress her cheek with my thumb before rising and unfastening my belt.

No matter how awkward it may be to undress with only one hand, I refuse to release my grip on her, so I shuck out of my ruined trousers and boxer briefs and pull on the scrub bottoms without letting her go.

She watches me with too many emotions to name. Pride. Sadness. Relief. Love.

I give my chest and abs a quick wipe down with the sponge bath items waiting on the bedside tray and towel dry before picking up the scrub shirt.

No matter how hard I try, I cannot let go of her hand. Even if she pushed me away, I wouldn't be able to release her.

I almost lost her.

Sorrow fills her expression. I drop the shirt and cup the side of her face with my hand.

"What's wrong?" I ask.

"I'm sorry, Giorgio," she whispers.

Tears spill from her lashes.

"Hush, *mia topolina*. You have nothing to be sorry for," I murmur.

She closes her eyes, shakes her head, and winces, reminding me of the contusion on the back of her head, but before I can call Dr. Karl back in to check her, she pierces my soul with her sparkling emerald orbs.

"I'm so sorry. I'm sorry I didn't tell you. You don't deserve this."

The agony shining from her eyes is too much. Despite the doctor's orders, I need her in my arms, so I slide under the sheet, replace her pillow with my arm, and carefully intertwine our bodies.

"You're right, I don't deserve you. You're too sweet for me. Too smart. Too honest and pure. But there's no way in hell I'm letting you go. I need you, Aurora."

"But I can't give you what you need," she says through a half sob.

"I've told you what I need. It's you. Only you."

She shakes her head and digs her nails into my shoulder.

"I should never have signed official paperwork, not without telling you I'm sick. If you'd known I was chronically ill—"

I release her hand and wrap my fist around her throat. When I tilt her face up to mine, the misery swimming in her soul shines through her eyes.

"I would have married you anyway, Aurora. You're mine. No one else can have you."

"But I can't give you an heir! It could take years for me to conceive, and even then, there's no guarantee I'd carry to term. The entire pregnancy will be high risk, and—"

I shift my hand from her throat to her mouth, ending her outburst. Fear and fury battle within me as I process her words. For several tense, uncertain seconds, she stares up at me as I fight the feral beast trapped inside my chest.

"You mean to tell me," I begin, half thrilled and half miserable over the fear in her eyes, "that you agreed to have my baby even though the pregnancy would endanger your life?"

She furrows her brow in confusion.

It's too much. I snarl, grab her nape, and duck down to take her lips, pouring my frustration into the kiss, more upset than ever before, but I pull back before my cock stiffens.

It hardens anyway. I ignore the stubborn *stronzo* and focus on Aurora.

As she recovers from my unexpected fervor, the slight blush on her cheeks contrasts her pallor, but her gaze remains confused.

"I don't care about an heir, Aurora. Those were my parents' demands, not mine."

"But—"

"You keep making me repeat myself, even though I've proven I'm a man of my word. Do I need to prove it again, *mia topolina*?"

"Prove what? How would you—"

"I love and need *you*, Aurora. You and only you. You come first, no matter what. If having a baby will put you at risk, then I don't need one. I'll prove it by getting a vasectomy. Hell, I'll get snipped tomorrow to make sure you're safe by the time you're recovered."

"But... the other morning, at my desk... when you..."

Realization spears through me.

"When I pushed my cum into your pussy? That wasn't to get you pregnant, *amore mio*. That was pure possession. Dominance. My inner feral beast marking his territory. I love watching you writhe in pleasure because of me, and knowing you'd smell of me all day long was the biggest turn on of my life."

My hard cock pulses against her warmth. With only my thin scrub bottoms and her panties between us, the heat from her pussy emanates along the underside of my shaft, but the fatigue tugging at her features strengthens my resolve.

Her wide eyes and soft *oh* will forever fill my heart with pride.

"We can pass everything down to Tristan or spread our assets to any nieces or nephews we gain down the line. Or adopt. I don't need biological children. I need you."

Fresh tears run across the bridge of her nose and drip down my arm as she studies my face. After looking between my eyes a few times, she skims her palm from my shoulder to my jawline and ghosts her thumb over the stubble on my cheek.

"I believe you. I'm sorry I wasn't truthful from the start," she whispers.

"You didn't know me before, but you do now, so answer me honestly. *Capisci*?"

She nods.

"Are you hiding anything else?"

She shakes her head. Stops. Closes her eyes and swallows. When she lifts her lashes again, my stomach bottoms out at the honesty shining from her depths.

"There is one thing I haven't told you yet," she murmurs.

I reflexively stiffen, turning her makeshift pillow into rock-hard muscles. She winces and presses her nails into my face. Her IV line brushes against my arm. The suspense steals all the oxygen from my lungs.

"I love you, Giorgio."

The surety in her voice and conviction in her eyes erases the tension from my body and ends the angst in my soul. I don't need to breathe.

I have Aurora.

She's no longer an Achilles. She's a Vivaldi.

My wife. My lover. My partner.

Mine. Mine to protect, cherish, and love.

We may live in a brutal world surrounded by danger and deceit, but nothing will ever hurt her again.

"Prove it," I growl.

A smile ghosts across her face as she accepts my challenge.

"How do I prove I love you?" she asks.

"Marry me," I demand.

She chuckles despite the pain of her wounds and the fatigue tugging at her limbs.

"I already have," she murmurs.

"Yes, you have, but that's not what I mean. After you recover, and you *will* wait until you're fully recovered, we'll plan the wedding of your dreams. I need to show the entire world how lucky I am."

She huffs a half laugh and closes her eyes.

"You just want to claim me in front of everyone, don't you?"

"I do. You're mine," I declare.

Her hand relaxes on the side of my face as she dips toward sleep.

"And you're mine," she murmurs.

As her exhaustion whisks her away, I hold her tight and whisper the words overflowing from my heart.

"Oh, I'm *all* yours, *mia topolina*. You're stuck with me forever. I'll never let you go."

As Tristan returns and settles on his cot, a profound sense of rightness settles over me.

My world revolves around Aurora, but Tristan completes our family. She loves him like a brother and a child.

I'll protect them both long after my last breath. With my name, wealth, and power, I'll ensure they live a safe and happy life.

No matter what the future brings, Aurora and I will tackle it just like we promised.

Together.

EPILOGUE

Aurora Vivaldi

IF EXHAUSTION HAD A NAME, it would be Aurora Achilles. No, not Achilles. Vivaldi.

Technically, Achilles is still on my social security card, but only because both Giorgio and I agreed it made legal matters easier and safer for Tristan, so now I have two last names.

I prefer Vivaldi, though. In my heart and on paper, Giorgio Vivaldi is my husband. I want the world to know I belong to him and he belongs to me.

Concern spears through me when I rise from sleep and find myself alone in the hospital bed. Despite three transfusions, a slew of other medications, and the doctor and nurses doing all they can to make me comfortable, I still feel like death warmed over, but the pain in my body is nothing compared to the angst in my soul when I realize Giorgio isn't in the room.

I rub the grit from my eyes. Confusion spears through me. There are no IV lines tugging at my arms.

Tristan softly snores from the cot along the wall. The low lighting offers me a vague picture of him lying on his side. I push my hair back from my face and grimace in vain, expecting tangles and grime but finding my scalp clean and locks brushed.

Soft fabric caresses my skin as I struggle to a sitting position. Looking down, I blink in confusion at the pink scrubs covering my body until my brain works.

Snippets of memories flutter through my mind. Giorgio and a nurse gave me a sponge bath and dressed me in clean clothes when my wounds finally stopped bleeding.

I don't know how long it's been since then. Pain and fear warp time until I wonder if it was all a dream.

The door opens. Giorgio and Fiero stalk in on silent feet. Other men hover like wraiths in the dark hallway.

Although moving stiffly, Fiero gives no other sign of his injury as he continues across the room toward Tristan. Giorgio flips the blanket off me and swings my feet over the side of the bed.

"Time to go, *mia topolina*. We've stayed here too long," he says as he tucks shoes onto my feet.

They aren't my shoes, but they fit.

I wonder why he even bothered when he scoops me into his arms and kisses my temple. My feet haven't touched the ground since Otello Tempe shot me.

He's dead. The man I instinctively hated my entire life, who terrorized my mother and murdered *mia tia*, is dead. Giorgio killed him. I don't know what that means for my family, but I do know it means Tristan and I are much safer.

The tense atmosphere seeps through my brain fog and slowly clears away my confusion as

Giorgio carries me down the hall and through the reception area. Shadows creep along the empty space and fill me with dread.

Several cars' headlights gleam in the front roundabout. A man dressed in all black opens the glass door and ushers us toward the backseat of the nearest vehicle.

Gunshots sound as Giorgio pulls my seat belt across my lap. He curses, abandons my belt, and pushes me to lie down on the seat while reaching behind himself and tugging Tristan onto the floorboard.

"What's happening?" I ask as I reach for him, but my husband cups my hip and grabs his pistol from his waistband.

"My uncle found us. Stay down. This'll be over in a moment."

He shuts the door and pats the side of the vehicle. The driver rolls forward until the car in front of us shields us from the parking lot.

Tristan lifts his head, but I push him down. He tries to rise again.

"I need to—"

"You need to stay hidden, Tristan. Our job is to be invisible. We can't be the distraction that gets them killed," I hiss.

His little body vibrates with fear and fury. I gentle my hand on his shoulder and lean down to whisper in his ear.

"Once Giorgio teaches you the skills you need to survive out there, I won't stop you, but for now, we're just a liability. Prove to him you're smart and stay out of sight," I say.

He blinks up at me.

"You mean it? You won't stop me?"

I take a deep breath before responding.

"I won't stop you. I trust Giorgio, and I trust you, so you should trust me to keep you safe right now. If he thought you were ready, he would have taken you with him, right?"

"Right," he grumbles.

Time stretches on and on. Each heartbeat feels like a million years, so even though the fighting only lasts a few seconds, my nerves fray and fear pounds in my ears.

When the door opens and broad shoulders fill the frame, I know it's Giorgio, despite the darkness.

"Are you okay?" I ask without thinking as I search his face and shoulders with my hands.

"I'm fine. Get up and buckle in, Tristan. We're going home," he says as he gathers me against his chest.

I soak up his strength as he holds me, and after a moment, an uncomfortable suspicion creeps into me, but he lifts me into the center seat and slides in beside me. He shuts the door and commands the driver into motion.

"What happened? Where's Fiero?" Tristan asks.

"Following my uncle."

"He got away?"

The incredulity in Tristan's voice reveals how deeply he looks up to Giorgio.

"You let him get away," I say.

He gives a slight nod.

"Why?" Tristan asks.

I connect the dots.

He's using his uncle as bait for whoever is behind the cyberattacks.

"What's important is that he and my father are no longer a threat. They have no power anymore," Giorgio says into my hair before lifting his head and directing the rest of his words toward Tristan, "so we just need to focus on settling you into your new room. *Capisci?*"

Tristan nods before going ramrod straight.

"Wait, you have a room ready for me?"

"I do, but you can change anything you want," Giorgio says.

"But you just said I could live with you the day before yesterday," Tristan argues.

I chuckle and squeeze Giorgio's thigh as I speak the truth.

"He's a man of his word. When he invited you to live with us, I bet he was already readying a room for you. When did you start prepping for us to move in?" I ask.

"The moment I realized you wouldn't leave the Achilles household without him," Giorgio responds. He pulls me tighter against his side and tilts my chin up.

"You're not gonna kiss, are you? Because I'm still an impressionable little kid, you know? I—"

"Precisely. Watch and learn, *mio ragazzino*. Worshipping what you love is the joy of life and your biggest strength, not a weakness," Giorgio murmurs as he lowers his lips to mine.

Every cell in my body wakes as he invades my mouth, filling me with delicious heat and turning the pain of my wounds into a tantalizing sting. I squirm in my seat and hiss when the movement pulls my bandages tight against the torn flesh across my shoulder blades. Giorgio lifts his head with obvious reluctance and wraps his hand around my throat to prevent me from chasing him.

"Not yet, *mia topolina*. You need to heal."

I sigh and curl up against him as his words drain my excitement to a low simmer, allowing my fatigue to take center stage. When he shifts uncomfortably in his seat, I study my husband's face in the passing streetlights.

Tristan said Giorgio made his declaration the day before yesterday, so I slept for almost three days in the clinic. Did Giorgio sneak away and get a vasectomy like he threatened? Certainly not, right? He wouldn't do something like that without discussing it with me further, right?

Except, as I study his face, the pain bracketing his eyes tells me otherwise.

I sigh again as I realize how stupid I'm being.

Of course he already followed through on getting snipped. He was dead serious when he said he'd do anything to protect me.

It's partially my fault for being so weak. Hell, I slept for three days. He had three days of staring at my pale and pathetic ass lying in the hospital bed to solidify his convictions.

Too many emotions hide within the realization, so I tuck it all away for later and wrap my arms around him, careful to avoid his bandages, and rest my ear over his heart.

He ghosts his fingers over my hip and cups the side of my face, holding me to his chest as though I'm the most precious thing in the universe. Tears gather on my lashes.

Less than two weeks ago, I planned to run away with Tristan and live the rest of our lives hiding from my mafia family, but now, I cling to the most dangerous and ruthless mafia don in New York City.

And I wouldn't have it any other way.

**

Nervous flutters fill my stomach as I study my reflection. The simple sundress looks nothing like the floor-length gown I'll wear next month at our fancy-shmancy 'official' wedding—which I'd happily skip. But Giorgio insists he must 'show off his beautiful bride', which just means he wants to stake his claim over me in public—which I'm oddly not mad about—but despite both dresses being comfortable, this one feels more like me.

Which is absolutely terrifying. The fancy gown is a persona. A shield.

This dress is me. I'm exposed, and not because of the sleeveless top or the hem teasing just above my knees.

The colorful pattern and simple cut fit my personality. It represents the true me. The sibling Tristan relies on, the sister-in-law Serenity adores, and the woman Giorgio loves.

I take a deep breath and relax my fingers before I crush my bouquet.

The door opens behind me.

I meet Giorgio's eyes in the mirror and twirl around.

"No. Out," I demand.

He quirks a brow as I stalk across the room and attempt to straight-arm him toward the door.

"Yes. In," he counters.

I gasp when he grabs my wrist and twirls me around. With my bouquet in one hand and the other stretched across my body and trapped in his grip, I have no choice but to stumble forward as he guides me to the vanity with his bulk.

He doesn't stop until the edge of the counter digs into my upper thighs. An inferno rages in my core as he slips his free hand into my dress and cups my breast.

"What is this?" he growls and flicks his thumb over the nipple cover.

I wriggle and stop myself from biting my bottom lip just in time to save my lip gloss.

"I can't wear a bra with this dress," I say.

"I know. That's why I like it," he murmurs.

He kneads my breast with his massive hand.

I squirm just to enjoy his hard cock rubbing against my back and respond in a breathy voice, "I also can't flash all our friends and family."

"But these don't seem very comfortable. Let me—"

He pinches the patch between his fingers.

"Don't you dare."

The breathy quality of my voice should embarrass me, but our reflection is more arousing than any porno I've ever watched. He towers over me in his delectable suit. I look so delicate and vulnerable in his arms. He could do *anything* to me, and I wouldn't be able to stop him.

I squeak when he rolls the patch between his fingers. My nipple hardens and pulls the pasty tight around my areola.

"What will you do to keep these?"

His suggestive tone and burning eyes melt me to my core. My knees wobble as he rolls my nipple again.

"Anything," I whisper, but I don't care about the nipple covers.

I want him.

"Spread your legs and lean forward, *mia topolina*. It's been too long," he snarls.

My insides throb. I'm still sore from two days ago, but my need exceeds my discomfort, so I shuffle my heels farther apart and lean forward.

He releases my breast and wraps his fist around my throat from behind before sliding his feet between mine and forcing them further apart. I squeak when he steals my balance, pinning my wrist between my thigh and the counter while holding me above the vanity so I don't squash my bouquet, and he flips my skirt up onto my back.

His appreciative groan skitters across my flesh and pebbles my nipples, causing a chain reaction in my core and clit. He hooks his digit under the string of my thong and pulls it away from my ass, tightening the fabric against my pussy. I whimper and writhe. The counter digs into my thighs.

"You're too fucking gorgeous, *mia topolina*. Brace yourself. I'll be gentle next time," he vows.

I mindlessly nod and shiver as he tugs my panties aside and presses two fingers into me. Pleasure and pain streak through me at the fullness, and even though I'm wet and ready, he works his fingers in and out of me a few times, stretching and preparing me for his cock.

His belt buckle clicks and clinks as he unbuckles with one hand, still supporting my upper half with his grip on my throat. I flex my fingers against my thigh. The vanity digs into my wrist, but I don't care.

A wanton sound leaves my throat when he presses the fat head of his cock to my entrance. I rise onto tiptoes, my body instinctively trying to escape him even though I yearn for his invasion.

The world bursts into a million sparkly colors as he fills me with one thrust. My entire body clamps down in a tremendous orgasm, and I soar amidst a kaleidoscope of brilliance as he ruthlessly takes me from behind. His demanding thrusts rule my world and reshape my soul.

His pace falters half a second before he surges impossibly deeper into me. The intimacy of his cock spurting deep inside my body releases the floodgates. I ruin my makeup and cry, needing the emotional release.

He sees too much. With our chests heaving and his dick lodged deep inside my pussy, he takes my bouquet and lays it aside before wrapping his arms around me, cocooning me in hard man muscles and surrounding me in his delicious, comforting scent.

"What's wrong, *mio amore?*"

He squeezes my hip and cups the side of my face as he meets my gaze in the mirror.

"I'm sorry, Giorgio."

He scowls and tightens his arms around me.

"Why?"

"You got a vasectomy, didn't you?"

His scowl deepens.

"Yes, I did, and I'd do it again if it means we can be this close without worrying about you getting pregnant."

I shake my head.

"But—"

He covers the bottom half of my face with his palm.

"No. The only butt in possible play here is yours, so choose your words carefully."

I swallow. He's serious.

A knock sounds on the door. I stiffen. He groans and licks my ear.

"Keep squeezing my cock like that and we'll never leave this room," he murmurs against my temple. "Tell them you need another minute," he demands.

I stutter out a pathetic excuse. Serenity asks if I'm okay. I give a lame response. She pauses. Commotion sounds from down the hall. Someone says Giorgio's name. Serenity chuckles in understanding before ushering the others away.

Embarrassment heats my cheeks.

Giorgio grinds his hips. I struggle to breathe as his cock hardens inside me.

"Did you forget already, *mia topolina*? I'm a man of my word, and I meant it when I said your health is more important than having an heir. I'll never regret prioritizing you over everyone else. *Capisci*?"

My chest aches and sandpaper scratches the back of my eyes, but I nod. He caresses my trembling bottom lip before trailing his fingertips down my throat.

"They're waiting for us, so be still or I'll start all over again," he growls.

I swallow and brace my hands on the vanity. He closes his eyes and covers my hips with his massive hands. After a few calming breaths, he pulls out and wipes up the worst of the mess with a few tissues from the counter before fixing my panties and tucking himself away.

He steps back and lifts me onto my feet before turning me around and wrapping my fingers around my bouquet. With a clean tissue, he dabs at my cheeks and kisses my forehead.

"Don't be late, *mio amore*," he says with a smirk before leaving me gaping after him.

With an annoyed huff, I turn and grimace at my reflection until my flushed cheeks and sparkling emerald irises outshine my smudged makeup. A small smile creeps across my face.

I've never felt so alive.

Without a trace of my previous nervousness, I fix my makeup and remain in a daze until I stand in front of the closed double doors at the end of the hall.

I honestly didn't know what my ideal wedding looked like, but Giorgio figured it out. When I hesitated so long Tristan suggested an internet café, my husband announced he'd decide where we would hold both weddings.

And I'm so fucking glad he did. With my mother in recovery and my father in mental shambles, neither will be here today, which is sadly another thing I'm grateful for.

I take a deep breath and push open the doors.

The heady smell of forest washes over me and the gentle sound of flowing water is the perfect backdrop for the view.

Giorgio stands at the bottom of a set of stairs in the middle of the indoor garden. Serenity sits on the bench near the fountain with Nico standing behind her and Camilla—who I re-met a few days after I recovered from my blood loss—perches on the ledge of the fountain a few feet away from them.

Tristan shuffles from one foot to the other on the opposite side of the clearing, but the flush on his cheeks assures me it's from excitement and not worry. Fiero, who I haven't seen in weeks, smiles down at my brother before lifting his gaze toward me.

Besides the guards surrounding the perimeter, I know everyone here except for the woman at Fiero's side, and I'm not sure what to think of her. She smiles politely until Fiero bumps shoulders with her. Her eyes spit fire at him. But the moment is so fleeting I wonder if the setting sun teasing through the leaves played tricks on me, because when she turns her attention back up the stairs, she's pure politeness.

Giorgio presses a button on a little black remote. The overhead fluorescents turn off and tiny fairy lights twinkle along the path and in the trees. Tears clog my throat as I realize he also tied small kites along the branches, mimicking the design on our rings.

With joy overflowing my heart, I meet Giorgio's eyes and start down the stairs. Almost safely at the bottom, I smile and loosen my shoulders, only to squeak in alarm as I miscalculate the last step. My bouquet flies out of my hand as I grab for the railing. I miss.

Giorgio catches me before I hit the ground.

When my heart stops trying to pound out of my chest, an incredulous snort escapes me at how perfect this moment would be in a fairytale.

Pleasure lifts my husband's tempting lips. The reverence, joy, and filthy promises in his dark chocolate eyes melt my heart. I hook my arms around his nape and pull myself up to join our mouths together.

It doesn't matter how many times I kiss this man; I'll always want more.

When he finally peels his mouth off mine and rises, I wrap my arm around his waist, plastering myself against his side, and give a dazed smile and head shake to the woman I've never met when she tries to hand me my bouquet back.

"I don't need it anymore, and you caught it fair and square, so it's yours now," I tell her.

She opens her mouth, but Fiero grabs her arm. She clamps her teeth together and glares at him over her shoulder.

Giorgio drags me forward, snapping my attention to the simple wooden altar.

His physician, Dr. Karl, gives a fleeting smile before beginning his spiel.

I haven't known him for very long, but Dr. Karl has already proven more capable and caring than all the other doctors I've had in my entire life. I don't know how Giorgio thought of him officiating, but it's perfect.

Giorgio pulls me impossibly tighter against his side. I squeeze him, demanding his attention.

He's mine. My ruthless mafia don. My trustworthy life partner. My husband. Mine.

And I'm his.

Always.

Join V.T. Bonds' newsletter for a STEAMY BONUS SCENE of Giorgio and Aurora as they settle into the townhouse together. What happens when she leaves his bed to sit in front of the computer? He proves he's a man of his word, of course!

Then come back and enjoy a sneak peek into Fiero and Emma's sexy and thrilling conundrum as the next couple in the Vicious Mafia Kings series.

TWISTED VOWS (PREVIEW)

Emma Lanza

I SUCK DOWN A DEEP BREATH, open my mouth, and scream.

He claps his hand over the bottom half of my face, cutting off my yell, and spins away from the dumpster. My vision blurs. I tighten my arms around my bag. Before I can get my bearings, he squishes me against the wall with his bulk and presses the back of my head to his chest.

I bite his hand. Hard. Blood coats my tongue. I gag, but bite down harder.

He snakes his arm out from between my bag and the wall, the brick shredding his sleeve, and pinches my nose, effectively blocking my airway.

I fight, bruising my knees and elbows on the building and tweaking my neck and spine despite his unwavering grip on my face and his unmovable weight pinning me in place.

Metallic liquid hits the back of my throat.

I release my bite, coughing and spitting out his blood. My stomach roils, threatening to expel my meager dinner.

He wraps his bloody hand around my throat and presses his palm to my forehead, trapping my skull against his sternum.

He's massive. I may be on the shorter side, but the way he towers over me is terrifying.

"Fuck, that mouth of yours is dangerous, isn't it, *mia caramellina*?"

His voice sends shivers down my spine. For a horrible moment, I think I've heard him somewhere before, but I shove the thought away and clamp my eyes closed when he leans down.

"Stop! I haven't seen your face. I can't identify you. Let me go. I won't say anything."

"Hush, *mia caramellina*. I don't want to hurt you," he rumbles with his lips against my temple.

"I'm not your little caramel, and I swear, I'll pretend like this never happened. Please, just let me go."

"*Mio Dio*, you sound so good when you're desperate. Beg me again, *mia caramellina*."

Continue reading *Twisted Vows (Vicious Mafia Kings Book 3)* direct from V.T. Bonds' website for an exclusive discount:

https://vtbonds.com/product/twisted-vows

THE ULTIMATE ELITES

A Dark Omegaverse Romance Bundle

What's better than a boxset? A bundle of 17 e-books from two series with alphas ranging from super soldier humans to alien ice giants, otters, rock monsters, hyenas, and so much more! Snatch up *The ULTIMATE Elites – A Dark Omegaverse Romance Bundle* and enjoy hours of dark and dirty filth. Exclusively on vtbonds.com.

https://vtbonds.com/product/the-ultimate-elites-a-dark-omegaverse-romance/

WARRIOR ELITE SERIES

Audiobook Bundle

Not in the mood to read, but still want the dark, delicious angst found in my books? Check my website for my *EXCLUSIVE Warrior Elite Series Audiobook Bundle - 10 Dark and Steamy Fated-Mates Alien Romance Audiobooks* and enjoy over 60 hours of growly alpha hotness.

https://vtbonds.com/product/exclusive-warrior-elite-series-audiobook-bundle/

UNKNOWN OMEGA (PREVIEW)

~ ⚛ ~

Seeck

REACHING THE FRONT OF THE ALLEY, I EXTEND MY arm and brace for impact.

She runs straight into it, but she's so small that I barely register the hit.

I snatch her out of the air, surrounding her with my arms, clutching her to my chest.

Before she can regain her breath, I drag her deeper into the narrow passage. My hand clamps over her mouth and chin.

Having her so close shreds my hold on reality. Seeing the wild array of hair short circuits my thoughts. Smelling her body and pain within my arms causes a well of need to burst inside me.

I push her against the wall and her cry of pain and fright dampens my need a bit. I meet her eyes and the world shifts.

Everything makes sense. She's mine. My own. My other half. My Omega. My weakness.

Continue reading *Unknown Omega (Alpha Elite Series Book 1)* direct from V.T. Bonds' website for an exclusive discount:

https://vtbonds.com/product/unknownomega/

RESCUED AND RUINED (PREVIEW)

~ 👽 ~

Craize

HE THUMPS TO THE GROUND, HIS NECK AT AN odd angle and his eyes clouding over.

Movement and sounds of struggle break my satisfied stare, and the agony in my chest pulls me further into the room.

A tiny form contorts on a filthy mattress, her white flesh blending into its surroundings despite her vicious lurching.

I step closer, my senses zeroing in on the figure, the pull behind my sternum demanding I reach her.

Pert breasts wobble and trim legs create the most luscious form I've ever seen, and even as my conscience screams within my hijacked mind, basal needs demand I take. Claim. Own.

I stalk forward and pin a slim ankle to the mattress.

Bright green irises pierce mine, abject misery shining from a face too delicate for words.

She's the reason I'm here. She called me.

Somehow, she reached into my soul and beckoned me into the pits of hell.

She's *mine*.

Continue reading *Rescued and Ruined (Warrior Elite Series Book 1)* direct from V.T. Bonds' website for an exclusive discount:

https://vtbonds.com/product/rescuedandrui ned/

THE KNOTTIVERSE: ALPHAS OF THE WATERWORLD

The Complete Series Bundle

*Light on plot, **heavy on spice**, dive into these 'quick read' dark dystopian human omegaverse romances knowing you'll find possessive alphas, reluctant omegas, and delicious battle of wills.*

Save time and money. Buy all 8 e-books now!

https://vtbonds.com/product/the-complete-series-alphas-of-the-waterworld/

Need something to hold while you read? How about something dead with my fingerprints on it? What if there were 8 dead things, all that have been in my grubby hands before? Try *The Complete Series: Alphas of the Waterworld Signed Paperback Bundle*. Only on my website, of course.

https://vtbonds.com/product/the-complete-series-alphas-of-the-waterworldpb/

SHADOWS AND SHAFTS (PREVIEW)

~ 💀 ~

Jennifer

ROUGH, SHADOWY FINGERS WRAP AROUND MY throat and weave into my hair, forcing my gaze to the mirror. I watch in horror as two sets of eerie eyes stare back at me, menace and lust emanating from them.

They tower over me with shoulders so broad they block out the overhead lights.

Bright purple eyes lower to my level, the creature beside me stooping to press the side of his face against mine. As we stare at our reflections, his smirk widens and he glances at the cat ears before meeting my stare.

"Look at you, little pussycat. Tiny and frail. Terrified and vulnerable. Delicate. We're going to enjoy breaking you. Fucking you. Knotting you."

Continue reading *Shadows and Shafts (The Knottiverse: Halloween Monsters Book 1)* direct from V.T. Bonds' website for an exclusive discount:

https://vtbonds.com/product/shadows-and-shafts-the-knottiverse-halloween/

RESCUING RED (PREVIEW)

>>> ✦ <<<

Blaide

"SHE'S AN OMEGA. THERE'S ENOUGH OF HER to go around. Why don't we work out a deal? One more won't make a difference."

A red haze tried to overtake Blaide's vision, but he pushed it away.

Calm. Detached.

He needed his head clear to save his little Red. These scumbags gave all alphas a horrible reputation. They had no honor. Blaide would enjoy serving them the pain and humiliation they deserved.

"You're not worthy of a single sniff of her, and I'm not in the mood to give second chances. Let her go before I annihilate each and every one of you."

They scoffed. Blaide sighed and rolled his shoulders. It had been too long since he'd enjoyed a decent brawl. Part of him was looking forward to this fight, while the other recognized how dire it was for the tiny female.

"Are you sure you want to do this?" he asked.

The blond scowled, insulted by the question.

Blaide launched himself forward.

Continue reading *Rescuing Red (Sci-Fi Fairytale Fusions Book 1)* direct from V.T. Bonds' website for an exclusive discount:

https://vtbonds.com/product/rescuing-red/

***

Have you ever wondered what would happen if the devil shared his witchy sacrifice with his pet werewolf? Lots of yummy filth, that's what. Read *The Last Sacrifice (Depraved Monsters and Decadent Myths Book 1)* for FREE ON ALL RETAILERS.

https://vtbonds.com/product/the-last-sacrifice/

***

How about a dip into contemporary BDSM? Get hot and heavy with *Sneaking In: Skylar's Story Part 1 (Deviant Doms Book 1)*, a dark why choose short story with dubcon, forced entry, and lots of dirty talk.

https://vtbonds.com/product/sneaking-in/

***

Holiday smut featuring an on-the-run angel omega, a sheriff elf in hot pursuit, and a biker demon caught between revenge and protecting the little angel? Doesn't matter what time of year it is, you don't want to miss this epic why choose omegaverse romance. Read *Knotting the Christmas Angel (The Knottiverse: Holiday Alphas Book 1)* now!

https://vtbonds.com/product/knotting-the-christmas-angel/

***

Guaranteed to leave you slick, each story in The Knottiverse—a universe full of nesting, knots, and morally grey alphas—has an HEA.

https://vtbonds.com/the-knottiverse/

FOLLOW V.T. BONDS

V.T. Bonds is a two-time USA Today Bestselling Author of dark and dirty contemporary, paranormal, and sci-fi romance. As a female veteran and mom of five kids, she enjoys writing filthy, action-packed romances with strong females and possessive alphas.

Go to https://vtbonds.com for a complete list of books by V.T. Bonds.

For new releases, discounts, and Knotty Exclusives, subscribe to V.T. Bonds' newsletter at https://vtbonds.com/newslettersubscriber.

***

Other places to follow V.T. Bonds:

Bookbub	Goodreads	Facebook

www.ingramcontent.com/pod-product-compliance
Ingram Content Group UK Ltd.
Pitfield, Milton Keynes, MK11 3LW, UK
UKHW031841100225
454898UK00011B/472

9 798230 263968